Title

Francis B. Nyamnjoh
Stories from Abakwa
Mind Searching
The Disillusioned African
The Convert
Souls Forgotten
Married But Available

Dibussi Tande
No Turning Back. Poems of Freedom 1990-1993

Kangsen Feka Wakai
Fragmented Melodies

Ntemfac Ofege
Namondo. Child of the Water Spirits
Hot Water for the Famous Seven
The Return of Omar
Growing Up
Children of Bethel Street

Emmanuel Fru Doh
Not Yet Damascus
The Fire Within
Africa`s Political Wastelands: The Bastardization of Cameroon

Thomas Jing
Tale of an African Woman

Peter Wuteh Vakunta
Grassfields Stories from Cameroon
Green Rape: Poetry for the Environment
Majunga Tok: Poems in Pidgin English
Cry, My Beloved Africa

Ba'bila Mutia
Coils of Mortal Flesh

Kehbuma Langmia
Titabet and the Takumbeng

Victor Elame Musinga
The Barn
The Tragedy of Mr. No Balance

Ngessimo Mathe Mutaka
Building Capacity: Using TEFL and African Languages as Development-oriented Literacy Tools

Milton Krieger
Cameroon's Social Democratic Front: Its History and Prospects as an Opposition Political Party, 1990-2011

Sammy Oke Akombi
The Raped Amulet
The Woman Who Ate Python
Beware the Drives: Book of Verse

Susan Nkwentie Nde
Precipice

...joh &
...Akum
...Test of Anglophone

Joyce Ashuntantang & Dibussi Tande
Their Champagne Party Will End! Poems in Honor of Bate Besong

Emmanuel Achu
Disturbing the Peace

Rosemary Ekosso
The House of Falling Women

Peterkins Manyong
God the Politician

George Ngwane
The Power in the Writer: Collected Essays on Culture, Democracy & Development in Africa

John Percival
The 1961 Cameroon Plebiscite: Choice or Betrayal

Albert Azeyeh
Réussite scolaire, faillite sociale : généalogie mentale de la crise de l'Afrique noire francophone

Aloysius Ajab Amin & Jean-Luc Dubois
Croissance et développement au Cameroun : d`une croissance équilibrée à un développement équitable

Carlson Anyangwe
Imperialistic Politics in Cameroun: Resistance & the Inception of the Restoration of the Statehood of Southern Cameroons

Excel Tse Chinepoh & Ntemfac A.N. Ofege
The Adventures of Chimangwe

Bill F. Ndi
K`Cracy, Trees in the Storm and Other Poems

Kathryn Toure, Therese Mungah Shalo Tchombe & Thierry Karsenti
ICT and Changing Mindsets in Education

Charles Alobwed'Epie
The Day God Blinked

G.D. Nyamndi
Babi Yar Symphony

Babi Yar Symphony

G.D. Nyamndi

Langaa Research & Publishing CIG
Mankon, Bamenda

Publisher:
Langaa RPCIG
(*Langaa* Research & Publishing Common Initiative Group)
P.O. Box 902 Mankon
Bamenda
North West Province
Cameroon
Langaagrp@gmail.com
www.langaapublisher.com

Distributed outside N. America by African Books Collective
orders@africanbookscollective.com
www.africanbookscollective.com

Distributed in N. America by Michigan State University Press
msupress@msu.edu
www.msupress.msu.edu

ISBN:9956-558-51-6

First published 2008

1

When she knocked she did not remain planted in the doorway but withdrew to the side so that anyone coming to open would have to stick out their heads to see the visitor. Kunsona opened the door and went outside, and saw a woman leaning against their wall in a tight white gown and white headscarf. Against the pale twilight she looked like a ghost. But the child was not afraid. She went towards the woman and looked at her closely.

"Who are you?"

"Your mother."

"No. My mother left."

"She has come back. The bunch of keys, remember?"

The little girl looked up at the ghostlike woman and discovered that her face resembled that of the woman she used to know as her mother.

"Your father my husband, where is he?"

"At work."

"Lead me in."

The little girl took the woman by the hand and led her in.

"Why did you leave us?"

"Shame. I was ashamed."

"Where did you go?"

"The shrine at Tabessi. The priest washed me and sent me back to my husband and my daughter."

The little girl did not speak again but danced out and looked up the road leading to *The Chariot Inquirer*.

2

They came for him that Sunday. He had just returned from a night's vigil on the mountain. He knew they would, sooner or later. They'd shown signs of late that they were interested in him. Nothing out of the ordinary, really. Whenever your time was up, they singled you out the way a lion isolated a bull from the heard and let the others go and then worked steadily on the hapless victim until it gave itself up as meal for the carnivore.

As a journalist you lived with your other leg permanently in confinement. You were picked up for saying too much, for saying too little; at times for not saying anything at all. Their dragnet carried no identifiable code. It was heaved and thrown by the whims of the force members, and it fell on you with the loose happiness of a mad lorry down a busy street.

Their cells had the conditions of Pollsmoor. When Mandela proved too stubborn, too dogged in his education of ANC freedom fighters, he and some of those he educated were moved from Robben Island to Pollsmoor in commensurate determination by his white gaolers. The cells in Pollsmoor were not single boxes that could hold three or four mates and in high seasons eight or nine; but kinds of little halls the size of an average basketball pitch, that could contain whole throngs.

The police cells in Tole were halls the size of a small wrestling field, their sanitary facilities, where they existed, just a tin bucket tucked away in one suffocating corner.

Inmates made sure they did not fill the buckets up too soon: the tin things were emptied only once a week. They protected that chance the way a child would guard a jealous piece of meat until he could guard it no more.

One week was the shortest detention time; so if the bucket filled up too fast, which happened rather often, the load remained in its corner for as many days as were left before the emptying time was up. When this happened, the floor took over as bucket and inmates pushed further and further away from their own remains into space that dwindled with the onslaught of odour and baked/watery deposits, yellow for the most part, but also pale green and even hot red. It was not unusual to see blood dribbling away from faeces as if from the neck of a freshly slain lamb.

Once he spent two weeks with them for uncovering an illicit liquor house. It turned out that the business belonged to a concubine of the Mayor.

This time they came for him on Sunday…

Church day…

God's day.

Why Sunday? Why would the Police pick anyone up on a day like that? Wasn't that just the day when men made their peace with God?

Sunday was a day set aside by God for His people, a day for them to empty themselves to Him hearts and bowels and all in confession and supplication, so that He could replenish their zeal for good and root out evil in their lives. Or did they think the Holy Bible and its moral goldmine was a joke contrived by some lunatics for asylum creeps?

He mused: These policemen are of the category of human beings who need God most, then he watched them in their professional seriousness, especially the tall one and his Chaka bearing. He could not help thinking: Their pockets are full of acts that should throw them on their knees before God. When you rape and murder, loot and plunder, should you not await Sunday with impatience, even with the anxiety of a guilty man?"

They chose Sunday. Which was just as well. He'd prepared for them. His mind was ready to be assaulted, his body ready for torture. It had happened many times before, and each time it'd happened his preparedness had mitigated the suffering. Police cells were torture chambers from which you emerged diminished, no matter how strong you were in mind and body, so you never allowed yourself to be dragged into them by surprise. You went ahead of the arrest, ran ahead of the brutality before the gun-butts and boots smashed into your skin; you gave up your blood before it was drawn, sacrificed your mind before it was defiled.

Whatever they thought they were doing as they came for him, he knew on his part that they would not get any more out of him than Mandela's jailers from the great man on Robben Island or at Pollsmoor. Brian Feinberg had done a wonderful thing by writing his little book on the South African legend. *Nelson Mandela and the Quest for Freedom* was only 71 pages long, but each page was an arsenal for the plotting and pursuit of the cause. The harder the gaolers came, the harder the prisoner fought. He could tell from Mandela's defiant obstinacy that courage was the mortar of commitment.

But giving up oneself to the forces of repression was not quite so easy as it sounded. There came a time when the body got tired, weary of brutality, and the other faculties, the mind especially, became rebellious to fortuitous assaults.

This time around, for example, he'd contemplated escape, at least until the storm dipped. But then the thought of exposing his family to wolves had had the better of his plan which now even seemed to him to be both puerile and selfish. He'd thought of boarding some crowded bus out of Tole by night and seeking a temporary haven in one of the cocoa villages on the eastern flank of the mountain that dominated the region. This plan had looked so attractive at the time of its hatching that he had actually packed his case and booked a place on a bus that was to leave Tole on a Saturday night; attractive, that is, until Kunsona had seen him zipping the suitcase and had said daddy let me zip it for you. Those words had made him look so stupid, so guilty really that instead of escaping he'd decided on a vigil on the mountain, spent in prayer and repentance.

3

Vigil…

How does one keep vigil, and for what? And yet we must. Whether on the mountain top as he did, or in the crumbling smoke-filled drinking places teeming with harlots and drunks, or inside the forest where once Simandu tore open the neck of his own son, we must.

Simandu. Rich merchant. Libation merchant. A lorry went in the wrong direction, that of Tignere, with kolanut load. The totemic python shed its skin in severance of blood link and in obedience Simandu marched his lone son into the forest and performed the rite. The head was allowed to hang from a tree-branch while the body was offered to the bowels of the earth. But the lorry never came back. It was not long before the double loss rose to triple.

We must keep vigil. Watch over the soul of the earth. Simandu's lorry never came back. Libation wasted. Blood lost.

Jesus kept vigil.

Munira did.

The day they picked him up he'd just returned from his own on Mount Bakingili, a mound of larva freshly unearthed from the crust of Mount Fako and pushed downhill to the brink of the Atlantic Ocean where it now sat on what had once been a flourishing palm plantation.

The larva was still warm underfoot ten years after the eruption of the main mountain.

He sat on a rock that had thrown its jagged face at him the way a bad woman throws her eyes at you and makes your blood heat up. The warmth trickled up the crags and filtered into his kaki shorts, through his kente jumpa and right into his hair.

A night of watchful thought draped in low clouds. How does one keep vigil over the soul of the earth? The sins are many. So many the stars in the firmament pale in comparison. The cup tasted bitter to its drinker. That bitterness has not gone away. The nightmares of brutality and stealing, of cupidity and murder, they all colour the flags of life men hoist everyday, everywhere. There's no more innocence; hardly any more generosity. Simandu took his son into the heart of the forest and returned alone.

The words of a daughter saying daddy let me zip it for you had driven him to the mountain where he'd spent the night with nothing but a thin cotton shirt to fight the penetrating cold. Thank God, the molten larva provided a warm sheath that took away some of the bite.

Vigil.

Avowal of his own weakness.

His individual safety. His escape. All that. And his wife and daughter. Did he for one moment consider them? The town would rise to news of his escape. Curious eyes would come and stand by the gate and peer into the house of the man who had escaped. And would exclaim: Here! He passed through this gate! I'm not so sure. A man running away will not pass through the gate. Yes, you are right. He vanished through the back of his house. Maybe he even stumbled and fell a few times. What does that matter? Coward. Just one big coward. His wife and daughter would become showcases of his cowardice. Did he think of all that? They would be questioned for his whereabouts. His house would be searched, his belongings - or whatever was left of them - ransacked, his wife, maybe even his daughter, abused. The real word was rape. Raped. It had happened to other wives and daughters for more benign offences. At times even for no offences at all. If Tendo was languishing in prison today, it had not always been so; only that the police had come - two reckless, tattered sergeants - one night, had asked him out of bed, and had raped his wife, then his eight-year-old daughter, with him looking on, mouth gagged. They had done all that and had slapped and kicked him in the face. Then proud of their act they had turned to return to their station. He'd fought the gruelling numbness rapidly and seized hold of an axe and planted it on the lower column of the one who had opened the dance of rape. The surviving one had vanished into the night and Tendo had been picked up the following morning and charged with the murder of a police officer. All of this because a barmaid in *El Dorado* had preferred him to the slain rapist, and he had been somewhat vocal in victory.

The horror of his escape plan seized him fully as he sat on that warm rock with his head raised towards the sky. He knew how violent Motine Swaibu could be in moments like this, when his pride was ruffled. The man's thugs relished such occasions. He just needed to snap his fingers at them the way a master snapped his fingers at his hounds at the sight or suspicion of an intruder. Hefty brutes, four, five of them, storming his home at night and ordering his wife and daughter to a corner before turning the place upside-down. He imagined them worked into a frenzy by the failure of their search and then releasing their carnal anger on his wife and daughter. He imagined many things. Each star in that night caught his gaze with another thought, each thought as bad as the other. Then he went down on his knees.

He could not say for how long he remained on his knees, but it must have been very long, for both knees were numb and bruised when he finally rose to the first cocks heralding a new dawn.

4

He was resting on his bed, in the book of Maccabees, when two policemen, one tall, the other short, knocked at the door. Bertha had carried his little girl to town, so he was all alone. He did not rush to open, but pressed on with his reading... *The inhabitants of Jerusalem fled because of them. She became a colony of strangers, and was a stranger to her children who abandoned her...*

The bang persisted, and he persisted too, his pace faster... *Her sanctuary became empty as the desert, her feasts became days of mourning, her Sabbaths were ridiculed, and her fame became an object of contempt...*

The knock swelled into a bang, still he read on... *As her glory had been great, so now was her dishonour, for her greatness was turned into grief...*

The frame started to vibrate, as if it would come off. No word accompanied the banging, but the power of the action told of their utterances if they opened their mouth.

A chunk of earth flew from the door-frame and shattered to the ground... Ah! If he didn't open they would do it for him, their own way. He closed the holy book away and dashed to the rescue of his door.

"Are you Shechem Nu'mvi?" the tall one spurted from inside a boiling anger. He did not answer immediately. Instead, he reached for his Bible again. The two men looked at each other, the tall one down at the short one and the short one up at the tall one, then together at him. The tall one especially was minded to wrench the holy book from him and fling it in his face or maybe into the glassware in the wall unit. The thought of the glassware shattering into bits caused his whole body to quiver. He closed his mind's eyes and heard the ware jangle under the sweep of flying pages, cutting wounds in the teak. A lifelong collection of painted glassware representing some of the best treasures from the Upper Adone blowers stood threatened with spectacular annihilation.

Let him do it if he cared, he challenged inwardly. Are you Schechem Nu'mvi? As if they did not know he was. Were they claiming not to know him? Who in Tole, save for strangers -really fresh ones - doubted the name Shechem Nu'mvi? That name rang through the streets and paths of the small-size town with the peel of a village church bell. That's what it meant to be one of the noted journalists in the town's only and popular daily: you found yourself in ways totally unaccounted for by your own will in the running streams of gossip, praise, criticism.

Small towns made big demands on their celebrities, quite often investing their hopes in them, very often too blaming their disenchantments on them. Take Makuiri's death by suicide. Not that he was not a strong man. He was. Accusations were known to break against his stamina the way a high wave would break on a vast sandy stretch. This time he'd failed to secure a place for the lone Tole candidate in the National Military Academy, even with all the money the town had gathered to oil their son's – and the town's - way into fame. Makuiri had dutifully handed over the money, all of it, to the Academy Commander and had returned to Tole confident that the town would soon be the proud progenitor of a military officer. But the list of selected cadets had come, and Tole had stared in disbelief. The look on the face of the town had been too much for Makuiri to bear, and he had sought refuge in death on a kola tree, leaving wife and three children to the cares of chance.

What a question.

Why hadn't they entered another house, any of those many plank structures that lined Tabi Lane on which he lived, and that looked like chicks of the same hen? Take the one across from him, Sabitout's. Its roof of old zinc was just as brown, both from rust and dust, its front hedge equally as likely to harbour snakes. Why hadn't they made their way into that one and asked its owner the same question? Are you Sabitout? They should have done that and seen how he would take it. Sabitout had not gone to school, but he knew where his rights were and on more than one occasion had stood up for them, victoriously. They should have gone to him.

Are you Schechem Nu'mvi? And this coming from elements of the Tole Police District where he'd appeared for interrogation so many times it was easier to check the number of days in the year that the place had not seen him. In fact the last time was three days ago when he'd been summoned in by the presiding superintendent and instructed - growled at – to stay clear of Juliana Diali whom everybody in Tole knew to be housed, fed and clothed by the same superintendent. He'd done an article on bribery in the police force, and his pen had dribbled in the direction of Juliana Diali in whom he'd caught a popular example of the evil that lay behind the greedy quest for money by officers of the law.

No policeman in Tole could feign ignorance of who he was. At least not these two, both of whom had been on duty on the day of his last coming and had scoffed at him noisily as he alighted from the superintendent's office with his face weighed down by the threats hanging over his life.

The short one stepped slightly forward. "Maybe it'll interest you to know that the other one has already given himself up," he said.

Well, if Levi was already in their net, what sense was there in continuing to hold out?

"He's already with us. He gave himself up this morning," the short one said, making sure the jubilation in his voice and on his face was not missed.

"Yes, I'm Shechem Nu'mvi. And what do you want from me?"

The tall one took back the initiative. He was a man with ambitions that matched his height, only that the enabling element of competence stayed far behind, making the management of dreams and reality a very irksome exercise for him. But having trained at the Ikeja Police Academy where faith in one's capabilities took second place only to faith in God, he had a faith in himself which not even eight years as corporal could dampen.

"Your identity is not in question. Mr Nu'mvi, you shall accompany us to the station."

The softness in the man's voice reminded Shechem of the chief tax collector sent to the cities of Judah by Antiochus, and how he spoke to the people with words of peace to deceive them, and when he had secured their confidence he turned round and fell on the city and dealt it a terrible blow killing many Israelites. He did not stop there; he plundered the city, burning and destroying the palaces and the surrounding walls. These two soft-spoken policemen looked to him like modern-day versions of the tax collector's soldiers. He looked beyond the soft words, which he did not allow to dull his awareness.

That's how they were picked up, his friend and colleague Levi Mu'tum and himself, eight months ago, and bundled off to Sanko Prison.

5

Levi was trailing his right leg to and fro on the ground and causing a light blanket of dust - mud baked by the sun and beaten into flower under the bare feet of prisoners and the thick-soled boots of warders – to rise to ankle level.

They sat on a little stone hedge, the remaining part of a high wall that, until two years ago, had segregated the women's quarters from the men's when Sanko was a mixed establishment.

To say the place was segregated was really stating it awkwardly, when one looked at the prevailing conditions closely and saw the kinds of things that happened there: pregnancies, births, abortions, many, many abortions, suicide by overdose, suicide by opening of the vein, marriages...one man one wife, one man two wives; even this case of one detainee pushing the number to four. Prisoners fell in love with the kind of passion that only risk exudes.

First the Administration cried enough is enough! hoping by this cry to exorcise the invisible worm. But no. The worm burrowed deeper. The love fiesta grew by leaps and bounds. Detainees sought ways of prolonging their term; like this one who punched a row of teeth off the mouth of an unsuspecting warder and earned himself a seven-month extension; or this other one who clinched his four-month extra time by breaking into the Superintendent's office just for the fun of it and with all the precautions taken to ensure that he was caught in the act.

The inmates had located the heart of happiness; discovered that where it was lodged had nothing to do with human judgment but with divine endowment. They had come to the knowledge that God gave happiness a heart the day he created woman, knowledge towards which the builders of Sanko had acted with sorry blindness and had erected a paradise in the place of a prison. Inmates had refused to leave Sanko at the end of their term. Even those who had not succeeded to contrive an extension had landed themselves in immediate return from the emptiness of the outside. And the abortion rates had grown in number and crudeness; and the rivalries had intensified, leading many a time to killings done in the cold anger of jealousy. Happiness and paradise, lust and blood.

Enough not having proven enough, the radical decision had been taken by the Sanko administration to bundle out the female population, source of all the troubles in the prison. They were sent first to temporary quarters in a rundown primary school become prison, then to a permanent site at a forbidding distance away from human habitation, a sight tough like Montségur of the Languedoc Templars. Only then had the prison administration discovered the key to all the mayhem: a huge hole dug in one of the walls separating the cells on either side of the sex divide: The orifice had been neatly dissimulated with smuggled cardboard painted in the colours of the walls. You needed to be a specialist in the art of transformation to detect the job.

From where they sat they could see the other inmates occupied with the same struggle to rebuild shattered lives.

"They picked you up just like Munira," Levi said.

"Just like Munira, yes. It's strange how the colonial ordeal sits unbroken on our continent."

"*Our* continent," Levi repeated, with a strong pensive edge to the adjective, then looked away sombrely. "Has the place ever been ours? How much? How much of it can we say belongs to us the way a thing belongs to its owner? The Darfur, Yupogon, Rwanda: that's our Africa. In those parts we engrave our ownership in blood." He stopped for a while, then said again: "You cannot own in bondage. We've never been free, unless in your infinite generosity you want me to believe otherwise."

"That's matter for debate," Shechem answered. "Freedom is a way of feeling. You see that man called Mandela? He was never quite as free as in his twenty-seven years of imprisonment."

"But that place is a stinking prison!" Levi cried in a mixture of affront and protest.

"Only Mandela's flesh entered it. His mind and will, hopes, all his strength remained with his people in the townships and docks, in the mines and in the plantations of the white people. If we ever come out of this place alive, remind me for the *Anatomy of a Miracle*."

"In the meantime, you remind me about the clipping of a debate when we get back in."

One of the inmates broke away from his conversation group and came towards them holding up two fingers fagged in a cigarette sign. Levi sent him back with a stern look, then resumed his talking: "My own way…it was like Karega's, except that they didn't get me out of my sleep but met me playing with my daughter."

Karega, Munira. Shechem had talked to Levi so often about Ngugi and his writings, especially *Petals of Blood*, that he'd ended up adopting the novel the way a barren woman adopts a child. He was not a particularly avid reader; in fact he confessed to some difficulty reading a novel from end to end no matter how short it was or how thrilling. But when it came to *Petals* the story was different. He admitted that the book worked a different kind of fascination on him: "The thing has a power that makes me feel I do not read it but live it." For example, he delighted in quarrelling with Karega, his favourite sparring partner, over the former's expulsion from Siriana. Why should a boy enter a prestigious school like Siriana and be thrown out for a silly strike, thrown out to swell the ranks of a generation that believes in charity? Where was the good example in such an attitude? On the other hand, he showed unreserved sympathy for Munira's little sister Mukami and her courageous act of suicide. Munira's penitence over his first sin with Amina the bad woman at Kamiritho was another bit he contemplated with thorough delight.

Amina the bad woman. Kamiritho or Kumba, the place didn't matter that significantly. Shechem's own descent into the sin of the flesh had been in Kumba and his own bad woman Bechem. The bush-lamp by the door, the dirty blind shredded at the edges, the bodiless face peeping out, the trained coyness of voice: pleasure ...that's all. The furtive glance about, then the dive into the dungeon. Coming out had been the problem. It was as if the whole world was gathered outside waiting to boo and jeer. The no-nonsense-end-of-business tone: I don't like people delaying here. If you could come in you can also go out... see other customers are walking away. Never slept with a woman before? The I...I, and then the damn-everything exit into a cold accusing street. It soothed him to know that somewhere across the continent - could it even be across the globe? - another person shared his sweat.

Above all a violent hatred welled up in him each time he thought of Ezekieli, Munira's father who to him was the most despicable neo-colonialist specimen. He did not like the man at all. A man who believed that children could be brought up on boiled maize grains sprinkled with a few beans and on tea with only tiny drops of milk and no sugar could not be loved.

"That man is a hypocrite and a neo-imperialist," he cursed, then screamed out a standard proof of his condemnation: "See... imagine this...he sacks a labourer for attempting to organise the workers into a union. Sacks him clean and clear and then denounces him in a church sermon! Bloody imperialist. The gates of heaven will crush his nose."

On the other hand, he liked Wanja... a powerful woman both in her beauty - or was it charm? He really didn't know and it did not matter that much after all - and her coquettish grip on men. To be a virgin whore was one of those feats found only in recondite writings. Men slept with her but never possessed her heart or even her body. She remained pure amid the dirtiness of her trade. Men hung to her smell in helpless adoration and were all without exception consumed by an insatiable fire of want. The more one slept with her the more one felt empty, unfulfilled. Was this to do with the fact of her being no man's woman and therefore no man's pride? Just when you thought you had her within your grip, she slipped through with airy ease, left you panting and gazing, and your pride defeated.

The bell announced the end of the recreation. They had it in mind to hang around again a bit but the stern summons of the warder on duty forced them towards their cell.

"Here," Levi said as soon as they entered their cell. Shechem reached for the clipping hesitantly, being as he was more for sleeping than for reading; but all too aware that until he read the clipping there would be no sleep in sight for him.

"There's only one submission in it," he pressed on excitedly, "that you may buy or dump."

Shechem remembered the TV debate and how he thought at the time that the proposing side were too cynical in their stance. Hindsight now placed the event in a new perspective and made a return to it quite rewarding. Without admitting it to Levi, he now longed to re-examine his own position in the light of accrued experience.

Should African countries be re-colonised? That was the matter at issue, to which the proposing side made the following submission:

The other day a friend drew my attention to a statement in a local paper to the effect that a Frenchman had just been appointed to head our national treasury.

Ladies and Gentlemen,

Should African countries be re-colonised? Put this way, the question gives the impression that African countries are independent. Totally misleading. Take this Frenchman at the head of our national treasury. What is he doing there if not telling us that our economic freedom is a pipe dream? We cannot discuss independence under such conditions.

How can African countries be de-colonised? That to me is the kind of question we should be asking. Re-colonisation and de-colonisation are separated by independence. Are African countries independent? Have they ever been? That is the question! We talk of independence when economic, political, cultural, scientific and technological self-determination has been achieved. Let us now look round and name one African country that satisfies this condition. We will all be hard put to it!

But what is colonisation in the first place? It is the act of one culture sitting on another culture. The former comes along with forces which sweep away those of the latter; forces like religion, science, technology, etc. It is the absence of these forces, especially science and technology, in Africa, at the time of contact with the West that opened the way for our defeat. Has the white man's victory ever gone away? For us to say yes it has, we must be able to point to a vibrant African scientific and technological culture.

Are we partners on the world scene or underdogs shivering out there in the cold? This rhetorical worry is proof that we are still a long way off. Is there any stronger ally of this assertion than the object of the present debate? We are as powerful – and therefore as independent, I must say – as our technology! No technology, no independence!

Ladies and Gentlemen,

Among the many definitions of 'colony' is this one that says it is a group of persons institutionalised away from others for some particular kind of care, treatment, correction or punishment. We can thus talk of a colony for epileptics, a leper colony, a colony of kleptocrats, etc.

This definition emphasizes the ethical mission of colonialism. It did not come to plunder and punish only: it also came to bring light, to heal. Do we have any reason to believe that Africa is a brighter place, a healthier place today than it was when the white man first came? At least the white man inflicted wounds under the soothing trick of religious anaesthesia. But see today. See for yourselves. What shall I say and what shall I not say? Genocide here, genocide there. All over the place genocide. That's the only thing we seem to know how to do. Our understanding of civilisation is fundamentally apocalyptic. We are not susceptible of grandeur! What have we inherited from our past? What are we going to bequeath to those of tomorrow? I leave the search for an answer to you.

As for me, the collapse of communism and democratic America's newfound power places African banana republics in an obvious perspective of re-colonisation. US President Bill Clinton made this clear in his January 21 inaugural address: Any fight for democracy is America's fight. As much as possible America will persuade, but she will also use force where necessary. Doesn't this sound like positive re-colonisation? I know quite a few people – among whom I count myself – who will not mind America's use of force to bring democracy to their backyard. We all know that the basic tenets of the political ideal called democracy are freedom, equality and justice. If democracy is the ultimate goal of intervention, then by all means let there be intervention! We should be wary of regimes that intone the hollow song of peace when they should be practicing the ideal of justice. Justice, not peace, is the pre-requisite for independence. Independence, that is to say de-colonisation.

Ladies and Gentlemen,

We are moving into an integrated world. The global village is no longer idle speculation. It is reality. So when we say we are democratic when we are despotic, the world knows we are lying. When we say our populations are well fed when our greed is sending them to skeletal deaths, the world knows we are lying. And a continent that lies has no place in the free world, in the de-colonised world.

As a continent of liars, Africa should be re-colonised, the better to be de-colonised from itself!

The incisive edge to this conclusion startled Shechem. He threw his mind back to the day of the debate but did not remember hearing these words in which he now found beauty, poignancy and truth.

To some, mainly the naively home-proud ones, re-colonisation may have sounded like a betrayal, but not to him. It was his firm conviction that the continent could yet do with some more white presence. He said so to Levi as he handed back the clippings to him. He could see joy…immense joy in the trembling hand that received the material, but he could also see a dogged sadness on his face caused by bitter experiences of humiliation. The instant miscarriage at the sight of a husband being spat upon; a husband loved and respected. Levi could not forget. Was that child girl or boy? He did not know. He would never know whether he lost a brother or sister. All that remained planted in his mind with bitter firmness was his mother throwing up as she reeled to the ground, and then the sharp cry of pain amid fresh blood oozing. The author of the miscarriage had walked away with his white hands folded behind him on his white cassock, and Levi's father had borne his wife away into their thatched house where the rest of the damage had been concluded.

For many days the catechist had contemplated giving up his assignment with the church. He'd thought of gathering his family back into the hills where he still owned a patch of land on which he could graze some cattle and goats if it came to that. The thought of giving everything up had grown bolder and bolder in his mind, finally taking such steadfast proportions that each time he saw Father Tinderman he thought he saw a thick chunk of evil moving about. But the power of the word had prevailed finally. The man had read extensively in Job, going from pain to pain, sharing the biblical sufferer's burden, so that at the end he'd decided against departing and instead built a new resolve to serve the Lord come what may.

6

They were not yet convicted, so they were quartered in conditions slightly different from those of the other detainees. Books and newspapers were delivered to them intermittently, even if under very strict censorship especially of content and title. *The Wretched of the Earth* for one was turned back as too revolutionary. To the guard who pronounced the sanction, the title was just a little too malicious and to prove his point, he'd opened the book angrily, crying: see!...see!...see! into every page, his anger rising ever more violently until he flipped into page ninety where he spotted the vintage evidence he was after and then cried further: here! ...here!, thumping the page angrily as he did so, before delivering the obnoxious finding: Listen to what you want allowed into this establishment: ...obviously there are to be found at the core of the political parties and among their leaders certain revolutionaries who deliberately turn their backs upon the farce of national independence. Revolution! Revolution! Revolution! Always revolution. Our hard-earned independence – a farce! Whoever this stupid ideologue is will not be allowed into Sanko. As for you, you can turn your back on our independence but one thing you will never do: turn back the hand of the clock. And let me tell you, everyone in Sanko pays homage to our flag morning, afternoon, evening and you will not extract yourself from that national duty.

Shechem could still remember the man shutting the book resolutely, then pressing his finger under *Wretched*, keeping the stubby thing there for long minutes, then moving it with emphatic slowness the length of the entire word, and finally fixing the bringer of the malicious work for explanations which, not coming, had earned him the full weight of the book as it pressed against his chest with an injunction never to reintroduce such offensive material into Sanko Prison again.

On the other hand, *Grace Notes*, Bernard Maclaverty's 1997 novel, the last thing he'd been reading before the whirlwind, had been allowed in with close to no objection. The book had been brought by Bertha. She knew his love for reading and so the first day she visited she made sure she brought the last reading along.

Grace Notes was admitted into Sanko Prison by that same guard who'd sealed the doom of *The Wretched of the Earth*. He'd found in the title of the one a musical appeal that provided a relieving contrast to the open hostility of the other and had waved *Notes* into Sanko Prison with the knowing ease of a well-read mind. But the musical ring of *Grace Notes* notwithstanding, its author had touched the story with the acrid language of indictment that bites all the more for being unadorned. There was one segment of the book that Shechem liked particularly - the one that talked about Jewish extermination. The area of the book that carried the episode had been holed by persistent thumbing, done in search of the clue to the deep trouble it inflicted on his conscience. Whenever he got to those pages his reading slowed into a ponderous beat that sent each word leaping at him with all its charge of blood and wrong…

"You knew Shostakovich?"

"Yes. Dmitri Dmitriyevich came here to Kiev with his wife number three, Irina Supinskaya. To discuss his Babi Yar symphony. It was very brave music to write at the time."

"Why?"

"You know Babi Yar?"

"No, not…"

"Maybe you are too young. Babi Yar is a place of death. In 1941 the Nazis made all the Jews of Kiev come together and they took them to Babi Yar – thirty-five thousand – men, women, children – and they shot them and put them down in a ravine to be buried. Evtushenko wrote a poem and Shostakovich put it in a symphony. But the anti-Semites said not all the dead are Jews. There is Russians and other prisoners."

'Hearing the words Babi Yar and Shostakovich Anatoli became agitated. He spoke to Olga. "He says they were all Jews who were killed. Dmitri Dmitriyevich was right - we must all fight anti-Semitism. The beginning of anti-Semitism is talk, is hatred – the end is Babi Yar. But, of course, in 1962 the State said there is no anti-Semitism in the USSR."

This conversation between Olga and Anatoli would remain in Shechem's head long after he'd read past it, and would intrude into other pages and disrupt his view of actions in them. Even where the action celebrated music and lighter human feelings, the pages transformed into a thundering red sea surging and billowing in a violent mixture of flesh, bones and blood. Thirty-five thousand human beings, men, women, children – just breathing things, maybe - lined up and shot, or simply gunned down with haphazard felicity. No question on crime, no worry about retribution. Only the pleasure of death meted, of death inflicted. The religious line became a searing rod that branded the unlucky ones before sending them to the point of no return.

Maybe if the State recognized that a crime had been committed, confessed it publicly, there would be hope that such acts would not be condoned in the future. But the State said there was no anti-Semitism in the USSR, which meant that the thirty-five thousand Jews dispatched to martyrdom would not have been killed if they had been discovered to be Jews. And yet they were killed precisely because they were discovered to be just that - Jews. Shechem had an everlasting problem coming to terms with the conflict inherent in State claims and State acts, as all over the world it was not what the State did but what it said in connection with the deed that prevailed.

Babi Yar was not in Russia and its victims were not Jews.

Along with *Grace Notes*, Bertha had also, on Shechem's express request, brought the unfinished manuscript of the book he'd been toiling on for the past nine years. The manuscript had no title; at least no definitive one. By turns he'd called it *The Second Round, The Red Stone, Tankeh Winjala*. But so far none of these captions had satisfied him well enough to sit on the book's cover once it was finished, which he hoped would happen in Sanko Prison. Maybe he could call it *Babi Yar*. Why not? Something about the name seemed to fascinate his conscience. There was in that name a mixture at the same time of mellifluous beauty and historical opprobrium. He remained captivated, chained, by the way the past could jump into the present, how a remote place in the Russian wilds could metamorphose into the nearest spot in anyone's daily life. Babi Yar. The whole thing sounded so beautiful, yet so terrifying. Was that not life epitomized? Existence captured in its paradoxical totality? Irak, Afghanistan, Palestine, Sudan, Babi Yar. What beautiful blend! But what terrifying symphony!

It was just about 4.30 pm when the afternoon recreation was terminated, but the cell was already growing too dark for the time of day. By 5 pm whatever natural light there still was about would go away and not return till the following day. The prison lights would then come on until 9 pm when they would all be shouted into forced sleep on roaring bellies and the stench and groans from the capital section.

Ordinarily, sleep came more easily to Levi than to his friend, but there were times - and this was quite often - when both of them lay tossing on their strict beds until the cocks in the Chief Warder's home announced the break of day. This was one such night. The prison lights had just been turned on and their first rays caught Levi's face from a loose angle, betraying a small ear and the outer flanks of a Ho chi minh beard.

"And to imagine that Motine Swaibu had his way with magistrates and lawyers and the police so easily," Levi said in his friend's direction, but without his accustomed joviality.

"Remember the bond that ties flies to fetid meat?" Shechem's words and his gaze did not both go in the same direction. His eyes journeyed along the bleak walls of their cell, spotting and resting on the smudge, much of it thick-layered and dry.

"Fingers of the hand."

"Motine could not have claimed innocence in the *B.O.* collapse, not any more than Judas could have claimed innocence in the betrayal of his Master."

"But at the end we were rounded up for pointing our fingers in the right direction."

"Clear case of the usurer hanging the cozener, you know; judge himself practising usury and then turning round to hang small fry."

"Is denouncing wrongdoing to be taken for the wrong itself?"

Shechem did not know what to make of Levi's question. Anywhere else in the world, a question like this one would suggest its answer with simple straightforwardness. But this was Tole, where wrong belonged on a pedestal.

Shechem did not say anything but just allowed his friend to get as much from his blank look as he could. His mind was taken up with the matter of their imprisonment. What ethical justification was there for their incarceration and Motine's freedom? They had already burnt up eight months of their life in Sanko without even so much as a preliminary hearing. Gradually they were settling into part of the prison's main features, just like the live wires, the maggot-jammed latrines and the clanging chains.

"You and I have lived in Tole long enough to know that crime, wrongdoing if you like, is not determined by the gravity of the act but by the social importance of the offender."

"What place then does proof hold in affixing guilt?"

"The proof is in the act. If the existence of an act is denied, how can you go beyond that denial to establish proof? Motine did not cripple *B.O.*, period. This very statement by itself renders all other propositions null and void."

"We were charged with libel on the person of Motine."

"Yes."

"But you and I know that as Board Chairman he single-handedly organised the removal of cash from the bank's coffers, first to a giant safe in his house, then illicitly abroad. We have the foreign bank account numbers and their holdings."

"Yes."

"You and I know that Motine as an individual is wealthier than the bank whose Board he chairs."

"Yes."

"And yet he is not a shareholder in the said bank."

"Yes."

Shechem's curt responses were beginning to confound Levi and he could tell from the way he held his lips at each statement that he was getting less and less amused at what he judged to be Shechem's cavalier attitude to such grave issues. He gripped his Ho chi minh and dragged it in a visible sign of tensing annoyance.

Lying down his dimpled chin in a neat mixture of black and white, the beard was spotted in memory of the Vietnamese leader it was named after. Ever since Levi stepped into Sanko Prison the beard had flown on his chin like a flag of identity, not least because, in addition to all the other things that had justified his wearing it in the past, it now convinced him that he was walking in the very footsteps of his idol who had spent eight months in a Chinese prison - flung there by a suspicious Chiang Kai-Shek - one of the lasting outcomes of which had been *Notebook from Prison,* a collection of short revolutionary poems that prepared the oppressed peasantry for the later onslaught on Western colonialism that culminated in Dien Bien Phu. Nguyen That Thanh at birth, later Nguyen Ai Quoc (Nguyen The Patriot), and finally Ho Chi Minh (He Who Enlightens), the great Vietnamese fighter was equalled on Levi's list of admired nationalists only by Ernesto Guevara de la Serna. But Ho bagged a small preference for the selfless dedication that attended his cause, a commitment to country so thorough that it left no place or time even for a wife or a child. Ernesto at least had two marriages and five children, and possibly a few other affairs that must have dogged the steps of his handsome figure.

"My dear friend," Shechem said, in an effort to draw even with his friend's growing seriousness of tone, "you are thinking logically."

"How else should I think?" Levi inquired. He sounded less tense now, even jocular.

"Just the way you are, except that your field of inquiry cannot be Tole."

"If it cannot be Tole, it can't be Motine either."

"Exactly."

The noticeable intention to conclude in Shechem's reaction was not lost on Levi as he asked no more questions; which did not mean, though, that he didn't have any more to ask. Levi was not the kind to let injustice off the hook that easily.

The son of an embattled catechist who'd been serving the Nyandong village church for forty straight years, Levi had grown up in the harsh conditions of a home that knew no affluence but that nevertheless fought off the trials that came with want. To maintain this balance, the children, seven in number, shared out into five boys and two girls, had been made to understand that everything in life had a place and a purpose and that on no account were roles to be mixed. Waste and graft were sins that Catechist Ezechiel Mu'tum took particular pride in combating. A man with that kind of background and upbringing could not understand, much less accept, that a bank could be looted and the culprit left unmolested, even hailed, while others were locked up simply for denouncing him.

"Not Tole, not Mo..."

The sudden clap of thunder drove the remaining words back into Shechem's stomach. A strong wind rose and engulfed Sanko Prison, causing window flaps to bang and cables and barbed wires to wheeze. The din outside now was deafening. Soon the rain came, the kind of rain that fell only in the month of May. It was both strong and pleasant to listen to, especially from a shade, best of all near a bed. Such rains brought back memories of those days when, as children, they would protect their heads with cocoyam leaves on their way back from the farm and allow the slanting drops to patter on the rest of their bodies as they marched on homewards amidst musical improvisations and catcalls. At times too, such rains would keep them under some big tree and there treat them to the chant of bushfowls and the shrill cry of crickets.

Sanko Prison was another setting altogether, what with its reputation as the cesspool of crime and evil, the beauty of a natural happening like a May rainfall caused only melancholy and bitterness to grip the mind. The absence of a bridge, however rickety, between crime and punishment in their own case deepened the gloom further, so that every other drop of the rain on the prison roof was just another turn of the knife in a hurting sore.

7

When the note came Shechem was taking his own turn at cleaning the toilets, which required pulling the overflowing buckets from under the plank stands on which users squatted, and emptying them into the ravine two hundred metres away towards the southern turret. The containers, thirty-seven of them, were lined out in one long hall, the zinc partitions of which had been torn down after the prison authorities discovered that inmates used the cubicles for other things outside answering nature's call. The zinc sheets were exposed in the yard for one week for inmates to take stock of their own filthy literature; and it was interesting how the authors themselves transformed into curious, even astonished visitors.

He returned to their cell later in the afternoon to an excited reception by Levi.

"Here," he said, holding the clipped note at him. "The warder slipped it under shortly after you left. The trial, I suspect."

He was right. The note was announcing their trial at the Tole Magistrate's Court in a fortnight. It said they were to be tried separately within two days' interval, Shechem first.

"They have finally made up their minds," Shechem said.

"They were going to, sooner or later."

"We are entitled to legal advice."

"I don't need it. Such services can only be a smokescreen. We have the facts, so why surrender them to counsel that may end up using them against our interest?"

"We shall assume our own defence then?"

"Don't we have the head for it?"

For all that reporting had exposed him to the basic iniquity of human nature, Levi continued to believe that the human being carried some residual goodness in him and could be trusted for right action. He viewed the biblical myth of the fall as a fallacy meant for no other purpose than to burden the human conscience with unwarranted guilt. To subject Adam and Eve to the daily temptation of the flesh was to him a much graver offence than the benign act of tasting of the fruit. The Garden of Eden was not the paradise it claimed to be - unless by paradise was meant a place of suffering - but hell where man burnt in the eternal fire of hunger and thirst, where man saw fruit of the most attractive kind but could not touch; smelt fruit of the most appetizing kind but could not eat, where man saw beauty but was barred from its enjoyment.

Armed with his cause-and-effect logic Levi thought it was enough for him to appear in court and proclaim Motine guilty of the *B.O.* collapse for the latter to be handcuffed and locked up in prison forever. Levi's was the kind of dazzling gullibility that blinded him to the difference between having the head for one's defence and being allowed to assume that defence in all objectivity.

Because the outcome of their trial was uncertain, Shechem elected to use the intervening time to round up his manuscript and have the project out of the way.

Levi regarded his friend's passion for writing with benign curiosity.

"If you had a writer anywhere in you I'd tell you," he cautioned with paternalistic gravity. "A good reporter, yes. There's proof of that...your many outstanding articles...Tole Slab Saga, The Biwume Wedding,...many more. Good material. But writing...the discipline...the demand on the imagination...you don't seem to me to come anywhere near those rigours."

And he was not laughing!

"Why don't you taste my palmwine before flinging it outside, calabash and all?" the besieged writer pleaded.

"I know you well enough not to need to taste your harvest. Your problem is that you want to emulate the writers you like... Ngugi... Knight and Lomas...by the way, see how you opened your arrest report? One would think one was entering *Petals*! But there's a difference between enjoying a writer and picking up your own pen in the hope that you'll be like him. I'm in prison just like Ho, but I cannot start a *Notebook from Prison* just because I want to be like that great Vietnamese figure."

"What stops you from trying? You'll be surprised at the writer slumbering in you."

"You are filled to the brim with visions of a master."

"And why shouldn't I? How are masters born? I will plod on, and rise and fall, and rise and fall until the day comes when I rise never to fall again."

"Ngugi the second."

"Shechem Nu'mvi the first, you should say. And think of being Levi Mu'tum the first. Think. That position is not for others only. You too can hold it. But if you do not reach for it, you will never hold it. Go for it. And remember, there is a price to pay, and it is called trials."

"Like this one we are in."

"Yes, like this one we are in. There is a reward at the end of this trial."

"With Motine Swaibu out there enjoying his freedom and telling the whole world that he will ensure our stay here in perpetuity?"

"Those are the words of a guilty man, as time will tell. Motine cannot get away with his act."

"This is just where your smooth thinking machine grinds to a halt."

"It cannot."

"Cannot?"

"Not so long as it is lubricated by justice."

"Whose justice?"

"Justice is not owned: it owns."

"Not in today's world, owned by the likes of Motine Swaibu."

"You are mistaking the dirt for the limpid water."

"The dirt…the dirt," Levi repeated in a voice leaden with sorrow. His mind seemed to have remained stuck, enchained to the thing and its stranglehold ubiquity. His mind's eye began to dart, as if besieged by a thing and its myriad forms. Wherever the eye turned, it came against this form or that of the same thing, hideous and howling, bloodthirsty, gangrenous. "The dirt," he repeated again. "You have hit the nail on the head."

"It is a symbolic nail; not one, but many."

Levi's eyes brightened. The battle going on in his head seemed to have swerved into a sudden spate of truce.

"Motine Swaibu is only one of many specks," Shechem pressed on.

"And a deadly one for that matter."

"A deadly speck of dirt," Shechem repeated, attracted certainly by the rhythmic ring of what his friend had just said, then added: "Not any deadlier than others you will encounter. It is in the very nature and duty of dirt to be deadly. As you can see, we cannot surrender victory to it, either here or anywhere else."

"I'm following you, but my energy is beginning to limp."

"It must not. Or Motine Swaibu will win."

Levi's eyes closed, this time very firmly. One could see tiny blood vessels dancing on the lids as they pressed against each other. The vessels were busy, as if they were conveying troops to battle.

A new scene broke into action behind the closed eyes. The things happening in it were not easy to dismantle and Levi was in them, marching, talking, screaming, hailing. He ran about a lot, and talked much too. He reached for figures, caught a few, but many of them either slipped off his grip or never entered it at all. Some figures also ran towards him and he hid them behind him and poured fresh drinking water into their open and panting mouths. But the ones he would really have loved to catch he failed to. Some of them actually danced tantalizingly close to him, so close at times that he could feel his eager fingers on them, but without the quick and tricky grasp of a trained catcher. They teased him in an appearance/disappearance merry-go-round so that soon he became dizzy and gave up the chase.

8

Shechem brought down the manuscript from the wrack three days after the date of trial was handed down to them. This was the first time he was touching the papers since Bertha handed them to him on her first visit more than eight months ago. The way Levi followed his effort indicated a growing readiness in him to discover the fruit of his friend's creative discipline and why not take a cue from there for a *Notebook from Prison* or any other title of his choosing.

"The title. What is the title?" he cried, with visible delight.

"I've not overcome that difficulty yet."

"Extraordinary. Simply extraordinary. Read me the thing and maybe at the end or somewhere near there a title will suggest itself to me that I can share with you."

Just then a warder stood at the corridor and shouted into their cell: "You both, not joining the other gangs for the morning chew?"

"No thanks," Levi said hurriedly as if to wish the guard gone from the corridor.

"As you please," they heard him mumbling as he strode away towards other cells.

"And now to our story," Levi ordered somewhat impatiently.

Shechem commenced the reading, his mind in a flutter: he'd been cut off from the world of the manuscript for so long that reading it was like discovering a new creation altogether. 'People were visibly excited,' he began. 'It showed on their faces, in the way they balanced the smiles on them, like bubbles they were afraid to lose.'

"Don't bother continuing." Levi ordered. The words froze in the reader's throat and his eyes darkened with failure and anger. Bad...bad...bad. Poor. If not, why would he not endure even the first paragraph?

"First paragraph," Shechem muttered, "not even my first paragraph?"

"It's nothing to do with your first paragraph, or the second, or any at all. Take it from me, you are no writer."

Shechem stared at Levi with imploring steadiness but gained only a very meagre concession from him: he would read the story on his own and discuss parts of it if he thought it necessary.

Three days later, shortly after a supper of chicken heads in salted water and clotted rice, they were back to the manuscript.

"The Katchi story. That's all I've found of interest," Levi said.

"Which is already very much," Shechem hailed.

"After winning the fishing contest, Banda is given two goats as prize. He kills one and names the other one Katchi. Why Katchi?"

"What does Katchi mean in the Nwemban dialect?"

"Net."

"Net. That's right. Like all the other people in the village, Banda believes that the gods decide who wins a contest. But he also believes that personal skill can and does sway the decision of the gods in favour of a particular contestant. That's why he offers only one goat to the river spirits and names the other one after his net. In fact, Katchi means "the magic net". The magic is more than just the power of craftsmanship, a lot more than intimate knowledge of the trade. The thing goes beyond all that. It lies deep in the heart... a belief, if you like... a conviction, a creed. It is anchored in the fibre of inner knowledge. You notice that almost everyone in Nwemba condemns Banda's decision. The elders say what he's done is a grave insult on the river spirits.

"Even their Chief orders him to sacrifice Katchi as well."

"Yes, but what does the brave young man do?"

"He stands his ground."

"Exactly. That's just what he does. Stand his ground. Tradition must surrender to innovation when the latter is in the service of progress. You can see that Banda refuses to allow his knees to touch the ground in his duel with the village council."

"One of the titles you toyed with was *The Second Round*. Is it to do with Katchi's rounds?"

"Yes, but more so with the second contest. The balance in Nwemba is still too heavily in favour of the river spirit. The villagers allow it to control their lives in ways that are unjustified. When they achieve anything, it is not their genius that has made the achievement possible but the influence of the river spirit. I want to use the second contest to change the order of things. That's why I give such a central place to the net. The people of Nwemba should invest in their nets, not in the river spirit."

"Investing in the river spirit is another way of recognising the place of tradition."

"Tradition that enchains the village to the immutable control of superstition must be checked; thrown out, indeed. No mind can meet the demands of modern day reality if it remains shackled to the limitations of superstition."

"What you call superstition is actually ritual."

"Agreed, Levi, but not all ritual is commendable. Genital mutilation for example is a ritual but you would not subject your daughter to it, would you?"

"It depends on where you stand in your consideration of the practice."

"Where would you stand to view it in a positive light?"

"Why? In the societies that practice it."

"Quite often human beings need to be rescued from their own folly."

"We are not dealing with folly here, are we?"

"No, but with ignorance, which is another shade of folly. Superstition - or ritual - as you choose to call it, is the nadir of the African condition. A people who believe in the existence of a river spirit will go to sleep where they should be weaving and trying out varieties of nets. The net is their capital, the beginning of industry."

"The beginning also of the end of a peaceful existence."

"Not until industry gets out of hand."

"As it does ever so often. It is never easy to say how far one can go in industrialisation and still maintain the required conditions for good life. Why would you want Nwemba to look like Tole?"

"Tole is a casualty of industrialisation. Nwemba can grow into a showcase of the blend between industry and quality life."

"But it's still a rural, ritualistic society."

"Even the most modern places on earth today were once like that. We just need to start by moving consciousness away from the river spirit and closer to the net and how it is produced. River spirits will not take us anywhere, except of course back into the river where only one thing awaits us: drowning."

"You, maybe, but surely not me."

"The river of darkness, that's what I mean. Remember what that speaker in the debate said? No technology, no independence. And I add: no technology, no sunshine."

"If I get you well then, Katchi is more of a symbol than a goat."

"Katchi is you and me. She is Africa vindicated."

Levi brought the discussion to an end almost abruptly, but then picked it up again with increased urgency.

"You say Tole is the victim of industrialisation."

"Do you think any differently? Tell me, if you suffer rather than benefit from a situation, can't it be said that you are the victim of that situation."

"Is that Tole's case?"

"Just as you say. Come to think of it: Tole is home to a shoe factory. One would expect at least that shoes would be the most affordable dress items here."

"A most normal thing to expect."

"But is that the case?"

"Not exactly."

"You don't need to be apologetic. *Not at all* is closer to the picture than your euphemistic *not exactly*. How many pairs of shoes can your monthly pay buy you?"

" Shechem, I didn't mean my request as an embarrassment to my dignity."

"Never mind. I'll answer the question for you. My monthly pay – all of it – is worth two pairs of factory rejects. I can only talk of factory rejects since that's all we're entitled to here anyway. You see, Tole provides land, cheap labour and raw materials. The mechanics of production and marketing are entirely in expatriate hands; in the hands, so to speak, of those who own the technology in use and control the market forces."

"Does owning the technology give them exclusive rights over the product?"

"You couldn't be more rhetorical!"

"It's not a matter of owning the technology. They are just greedy racists. They think shoes are good for their feet only. We don't have feet, so what do we need shoes for?"

Owning technology, racists, feet and shoes…

Coming from Levi, that accusation was not surprising. He had a morbid hatred for the white man resulting from the hardened layers of contradiction and humiliation his life as the child of a catechist had exposed him to, either directly – as when a white priest once tried to abuse him sexually – or vicariously when on several occasions he witnessed his father's ears being pulled by a white priest for no other reason than that he took too long in counting the Sunday collections. In fact he'd seen a priest spit in his father's face once, and since that incident he had gone through life bearing the dregs of the white man in his skin. He could not think of a stronger evil than this one in which one human being was made to bear the scum of another human being simply because the mistakes of history had established an up/down relationship between them.

Mistakes of history? The question needed clarification. Was it the mistakes of history that placed white people up and black people down? Wherever you went and saw these two races together, that same immutable order stared you in the face, unwritten, unspoken, silent, but there. It could not be an accident.

Louis James thought the linking of the symbolic values of black and white to the colour of the skin was a twentieth-century accident induced by a peculiar historical situation. What accident and what peculiar historical situation was he thinking of? Slavery? Possibly. A lecturer in English at the University of Kent at Canterbury, he was too much of a humanist thinker, too much of a later-day Chaucer, to see race relations in any context outside the moral. His own tenet was that in each of us the moral valuation by which 'white' became good and 'black' evil had to be continually challenged by the inchoate, creative world in which dark represented vitality, good, and white lack of life, evil.

Thank God there were not many to think like him! Frankly, who was the English thinker trying to fool? How did he want anyone in his right senses to see good and vitality in black, and evil and death in white? That would be like turning the tide of the Sahara desert tragedies with a north-south migratory trend. Absolute claptrap.

Symbolic values. That made more sense. But then, outside the river spirits, what other symbolic values could one think of that pertained to black people? Values that were intrinsically theirs, values authored by their own native genius? Communalism? Make-belief, all that. African societies were more individualistic than could ever be imagined. Technology? Science? These two were as white in their origins as the Kalahari desert was black in its dryness. There was no greater essence to white values than the twin essence of science and technology. Could such thinking clear his friend's mind and resolve once and for all the contradiction that had driven him into silence?

"Mr Levi you see, the prime mover of racism is technology."

At this, Levi crackled his fingers in a flurry that jarred in Shechem's ears, then turned a determined look towards him: "This is a matter of plain talk, not sophistry. Racism is skin."

"Mr Levi, I beg to insist: racism is sense. The skin only helps in the outer identification of a deeper ordering."

"How is that?"

"Listen. When a white man calls you a nigger he means this mass of flesh that cannot think, not this thinking man with black skin. Your being black is immaterial. Blackness is even an asset. An aesthetic asset."

"Don't serve me that sweet-coated nonsense."

"Neither one nor the other, you can be sure. Your biggest liability is the emptiness of your head, technologically speaking. In fact, I can go even further and say the world doesn't exist."

"Now you are getting really interesting!" Levi said, then rose to his feet and flexed out his right knee to let go sounds like dry wood breaking. "The world doesn't exist." This one he said with the dismay of a man witnessing the beginnings of madness.

"I will say the same thing again. The world doesn't exist. Only interests do. Races do not exist. Only interests do. And the engine of these interests is technology." Shechem did not look at Levi's face to see whether he was following or not, but just pressed on as if he was addressing an imaginary audience. "That was what I meant when I said Nwemba had to turn its mind away from the river spirit to nets and their production. So long as we do not domesticate technology we will continue, like Tole, to be waste disposal points in this age of technology. We can buy planes and mobile phones and what else have you, but we will continue to remain users, not makers. The world is in the hands of the latter category; let's not be fooled on that score."

"I admire the empirical straightforwardness of your argument," Levi applauded, "but I think it still stands to reason that in a world that makes so much ado about humanism and the basic equality of the races, technology should not be allowed to shut out the imperatives of mutual regard."

"Emotional talk. Think...don't only think...reason. Reason. How much regard do you want an MIT-trained white man to have for a creature in the Kalahari desert?"

"As if he had any more for an MIT-trained black man!"

"And why's that? Or are you too busy being angry with the white man to see the logic of his action?"

The response was a gruff face.

"Race tag, ever heard of that? The educated black man does not suffer as an individual; he suffers as a type. Your MIT-trained black man is perceived as an intruder into a technological culture his race has done nothing to bring about. Think of a white man dancing *makossa* or *bikutsi*. No matter how beautifully he does it, he remains an intruder. He can never be viewed in intrinsic terms as far as those rhythms go. He can never totally appropriate them because they are alien to his roots. I think that's the point. Technology is alien to black roots. That's why all our technological ventures wither so easily. They lack roots. They are without the sanction of ancestry. We copy, we don't originate...we don't father...we don't give birth to. We're just there waiting for the pear to fall on our heads to pick and eat, repeating the robotic gesture over the centuries without ever asking the kind of question that could lead us too to Newton's gravitational hurrah! "

Levi did not utter a word. And yet Shechem thought, judging from the provocative weight of his reflection, that Levi would assail him with traditional arrows meant to dislodge his technological anchors. In fact there was a yearning look on his face thirsting for more knowledge and greater insight. The biting insults in Shechem's utterances seemed instead to be having a therapeutic effect on his friend; to be washing away the soot from his eyes. The refutation of skin-based racism seemed to have shaken the basic pillar of Levi's worldview. Shechem moved in like a boxer who had opened a deep cut in his opponent's eye and was about to punch the face blind with the blood of victory.

"These things I tell you have lain deep in me for many years, put there by Frantz Fanon. If there's any one man who knows the psychology of human relations, that man is Frantz Fanon. *The Wretched of the Earth* is not just a book like any other book. It is the ultimate therapeutic document for all underprivileged peoples, for it tells them what to do in order to attain the dimension of full humanity. This is what you find on pp. 48 and 49 of that book: The oppressed peoples *have remained in the same childish position as Engels took up in his famous polemic with the monument of puerility, Monsieur Dûring: In the same way that Robinson (Crusoe) was able to obtain a sword, we can just as well suppose that (Man) Friday might appear one fine morning with a loaded revolver in his hand, and from then on the whole relationship of violence is reversed: Man Friday gives the orders and Crusoe is obliged to work…Thus, the revolver triumphs over the sword, and even the most childish believer in axioms will doubtless form the conclusion that violence is not a simple act of will, but needs for its realization certain very concrete preliminary conditions, and in particular the implements of violence; and the more highly-developed of these implements will carry the day against primitive ones. Moreover, the very fact of the ability to produce such weapons signifies that the producer of highly-developed weapons, in everyday speech the arms manufacturer, triumphs over the producer of primitive weapons. To put it briefly, the triumph of violence depends upon the production of armaments, and this in its turn depends on production in general, and thus….on economic strength, on the economy of the State, and in the last resort on the material means which that violence commands…*

"This is it, Levi. The logic of human relations cannot be stated more concisely. As you can see, Engels does not dwell on the colour of Crusoe's skin, or for that matter on that of Man Friday. He is interested in their inventiveness, in their power to produce the weapons that give them control over man and nature. The existential clash is not between black and white, but between developed weapons and primitive weapons, between technology and its absence."

A weight seemed to have fallen from Levi's shoulders for he rose from near the window where he'd been standing and went over to Shechem's bed. The setting sun threw his thin shadow ahead of him so that Shechem was overwhelmed by the sense of touch even before he was touched. When he came close he seized Shechem by the shoulders and lifted him to his feet, fixing him in the eyes.

"Shechem," he said, holding him more and more firmly, "the educated black man suffers as a type. You mean it was not on my father that Tinderman spat but on the black man in him? You mean there is yet some dignity spared for Ezechiel Mu'tum?"

Shechem offered no response. The question was in itself its most resounding answer. A new vista seemed to have thrown itself open to

Levi down which his understanding of race relations underwent a salutary transformation. By throwing off the burden of hatred that had clogged his chest, he had cleared the way for nobler feelings and healthier rapports. Although Tinderman had long since returned to his native Holland, he would reach out to him by mail or, failing that, in prayers. He would pray for him, steadfastly. Yes, that was what he would do. He would ask God in his supplication to forgive Father Tinderman for spitting on his father. At the time of the incident he'd not been armed with the kind of understanding he now had. He saw things differently now. For example, he now understood that there were always two people in a black man and that the two were perforce supportive of each other, even if at times too they fell out with each other, especially when the civilized one was punished in place of the primitive one, made to endure atavistic persecution, that is.

"Levi," Shechem said when he thought Levi had held him long enough to come to terms with himself, "we must never forget that our shadow is actually the duplicate projection of ourselves from which we can never flee. We have the duty to make shadow and substance one, as the white man has done in his own case. The primitive white man has been absorbed by the civilized white man so that even his most primitive acts are still viewed with some civilised compassion. That's what we should work towards. The civilized man in us must swallow up the primitive man so that when the white man sees us he should respect us, not spit on us."

"We spit on ourselves more often than the white man does," Levi said.

"How's that?" Shechem questioned, as if in ignorance but in actual fact thoroughly surprised at the sudden profundity of his friend's thinking.

"Just see where we are. What are we doing here? What has Motine done if not spit in our faces?" At this he seized his left jaw as if to feel the slimy dirt on it.

The question was both startling in terms of its author and revealing of his new sense of penetration. The things that had bedevilled Levi's childhood experience and made him into a bitter young man he now viewed and accommodated with maturity.

"He has done a lot worse than spit in our face," Shechem said. "He has confirmed our nothingness. This is a much more devastating act than the physical one of flying dirty spittle at our face."

"He has confirmed our nothingness," Levi repeated, like a pupil after his master in a classroom, then said in a way that underlined his mature understanding of what he had just repeated: "I like the beauty of the statement and the ugliness of its message."

“That’s the paradox of our station,” Shechem said, in a visible effort to draw even with his friend’s philosophical flight. “We are very good at destroying our own image.”

“Is the we the individual or the type, may I ask, borrowing from your lexicon.”

“And what do you think it is if not the type?”

“The type, surely. Motine Swaibu, more type than individual. He does what the race is best known for. He belittles. He travesties. He lies. He destroys. See what he and his friend Dan Mowena have turned the machinery of justice into.”

“And with that we expect the outsider to respect us. Tell me, if a white man comes here now and spits in the face of a magistrate, will you take offence?”

“Not ever since you opened my eyes to the duality of the black man’s existence.”

“But if he came here and discovered that our judiciary was upright, that crime was punished, systematically, and innocence vindicated, what would he do?”

“Doff his hat, of course.”

“Once again, the responsibility is ours, not that of the outsider.”

“Poor Tole!” Levi exclaimed, as if crushed by the size of the job ahead.

9

Levi and his friend reported for *The Chariot Inquirer*, the only daily in the town. The former had been with the paper for eight years, the latter for slightly more, maybe nine.

Shechem had no formal training as a journalist; rather, he was what one could term a jack. He'd joined the paper from three years of street life after a B.Sc. degree in sociology and anthropology from a Nigerian university, and two months after Bertha gave him Kunsona, his first and to this day only child.

His family occupied a three-bedroom plank bungalow on Tabi Lane, a middle-income neighbourhood situated on the southside of Tole, one hour's walk from *The Chariot* offices. His was a very small family, composed only of Bertha, Kunsona and himself. But if you were not told of the tiny number of inhabitants of the home, you would think after five or so minutes in front of the house on a normal evening that you were in front of a football stadium hosting a cup final. Kunsona for one was a boisterous little being in whose presence all household utensils and moveable furniture transformed into ufos. The only furniture piece that had stood up to her King Kong sprees was the 1936 radiogram he'd acquired at an auction and had stowed away on the wall unit, within sight quite all right, but out of reach. Several times she'd contrived a babelian ladder to reach it but had given up after three successive crashes, each of which had earned her only a "serves you right" compliment from her mother.

Kunsona's liveliness of limb met an equal match in her mother's own chaotic liveliness of voice. Bertha took triumphant pride in her gifts as a singer, and made a proud show of them. She sang in the kitchen, sang in the bathroom, sang in the yard, sang in the living room, sang most joyously in the bedroom; and when she was not singing - which happened very rarely while she was awake - she was yelling at Kunsona- which was quite often given the frequency with which she and Kunsona's ufos made encounters of the third order.

It was always his favourite philosophy that habit, especially when driven by genuine affection, transformed fortitude into pleasure. And it worked well with him. By nature he was taciturn and more of a recluse. Those who knew him even complained of his exaggerated taste for loneliness. Many said he and Bertha were too disparate to live under one roof, let alone as man and wife, and saw in their wedding the celebration of difference, not the cementing of harmony. But the predicted rocks never solidified. Instead, he grew so used to her ways that if you took her away from him you also took away his life force. The birth of Kunsona and the hilarious pleasure he derived watching her grow up, this coupled with his wife's place in his life, had been the biggest reward he'd received from God.

The paper and his home were the two extremities between which his life radiated. If he was not in one he was in the other and both procured him comparable even if different sweeps of joy.

Every day of the week the paper sent out reporters and investigators to comb the main streets and back streets of Tole for news items, by which was meant anything worth talking about. And a town like this one whose rhythm was dictated by the shoe factory, the bank and the many drinking spots gave any reporter worth his salt a permanent professional field day.

At first the townspeople balked at so much scrutiny, but gently and as time passed they grew used to it and finally accepted it. But far from being a welcome, that acceptance was resignation to a practice they could not change or halt.

General opinion in Tole had held it for quite a time that the two young man were taking the law a bit too much into their hands by digging up spicy happenings, with little or no regard for how their acts affected people's standing in the town. The truth is that they considered no man too big, no incident too insignificant to be reported on; that being their business - reporting.

That was how, quite naturally, when news started reaching them that the foundation of the *Beautyful Ones* was beginning to develop cracks at its edges they turned their attention to it.

By ordinary standards *B.O.* was a small-size venture, with its staff strength of twenty-six and capital deposit of forty million CFA francs. Its main customer pool was the shoe factory workers who for the most part fell in the medium and low-income bracket. The factory management ran a social insurance scheme also housed with the bank.

Besides these fixed partners, there were the many individuals who starved both self and family to feed their passbook, mite on mite, till a substantial sum grew out of their steadfast abnegation.

"What's the weight of your passbook?" was the challenge that no man in Tole allowed to go unanswered; unless he was not a man, thrift being their next best passion after their work.

Everyone called *B.O.* the financial octopus of Tole and there was no day like payday in the town to empty the full weight of this metaphor on the life of the town. On this, the last day of the month, Tole vomited the bulk of its workers on the glassed rectangular building dug into the side of the town's lone rise. Workers in colourfully dyed Benin wax jumpas streamed to the bank like worshippers flocking to church on Sunday, then queued before the main glass door and waited patiently for their names to be called for them to go in and receive their pay, much of which they left behind to consolidate their passbook.

No matter the flow of customers, all of them were attended to before it was midday and the trickle of the last customers was always an indication of business having been conducted successfully. The shutters then came down and sealed the money house off in a kind of mystery that was both enchanting and awesome.

But gently, the shutters started coming down further and further away from midday. One payday they didn't come down at all the whole day, and the queue remained, long and stoic, until evening. To while away time customers broke into little conversation groups, but not without putting down their passbooks on the ground to indicate their place on the queue.

Most of them sat on the escarpment to the left side of the bank and talked against a sky that washed them with colours of blue and patches of thick white announcing the impending rain. They talked about the factory, how it overworked them for little money; some talked with particular bitterness about the white man who came in once every month and carried away cartons of money and drove off in his khaki-coloured jeep leaving behind thick bands of dust; quite a few complained of not knowing the white man's name and of how they were instructed never to discuss him in the factory premises.

They talked with their eyes all the time on the bank shutters and on their passbooks on the ground. Occasionally a wind blew away a passbook or opened a page and exposed the neatly-crafted figures to the burning sun. Bringing the blown passbooks back into place and closing the open ones helped to chase away the time, but the sport did only a poor job in hiding the anxiety that sat more and more firmly on their faces as the bank shutters refused to come down.

Levi followed the events sitting in front of a beer on the veranda of *El Paso*, then felt his way into his friend's house late in the evening to announce that all was not well with *B. O.*, thus blowing the lid off the pandora's box that the bank had become.

In the most dramatic piece of reporting yet seen in the pages of *The Chariot Inquirer* the two journalists, known for their investigative acumen, proved that Motine Swaibu, Tole's leading tycoon, had crippled the bank during his term of office as its Board Chairman. In an equally dramatic legal *tour de force* Motine demonstrated that not only had he no hand in the bank's collapse, he was even the most aggrieved party in the entire mishap, having lost not less than eight million francs in savings and other deposits. With his innocence demonstrated and underwritten by a limping judiciary, he'd had no trouble obtaining the arrest and incarceration of what he termed 'the two injurious reporters'.

This was eight months ago. The trial was now just two weeks off. Shechem knew that Motine would stop at nothing to keep them in prison forever, so he drove the need for legal counsel home to Levi. His friend saw things the way he did and two days later Barrister Ekobena held a first briefing meeting with them at the end of which he was sufficiently convinced by their case to want to take up their defence.

But the Barrister concluded the meeting with the hint that he'd solicit an amicable settlement with the plaintiff and appear in court only if that attempt failed.

"Your chances of defeating Motine Swaibu in Justice Dan Mowena's court are lean, not to say inexistent," he said in explanation. "I've been to see the Justice who wasted no time to tell me of his firm intention to hear the case himself. He accused the two of you of highhandedness. 'Those two think they are above the law,' were his exact words."

"What makes you think we'll not have a fair hearing in that court?" Levi queried.

"Courts are my place of trade as you know, just as the back streets of Tole are yours. Courts here are not institutions; they are persons. The person is the court. What he likes the court likes; what he hates the court despises."

Shechem knew the situation only too well, so he didn't bother to join in the discussion.

"Granted," Levi persisted, "but Dan Mowena has no axe to grind with us."

"He may not, but Motine Swaibu is his bosom friend; I'd even say partner. You see the turn in the road?"

"If such be the case Mowena is an interested party and should therefore not hear the matter."

"It is precisely because he is an interested party that he wants to hear the matter. There's so much at stake in it for him!"

"Would an amicable settlement not be a travesty?"

"Sure, but then is your own incarceration not one, Shechem?" Ekobena said, turning to him. "Your comrade here continues to think that Tole is a spot on earth where the gangrenes don't penetrate. The disenchantments in our trade are daily and many. We sow justice but what we reap is almost always its negation."

These were the words Ekobena wanted to plant in the minds of the two journalists. Coming ahead of their trial, the words were not of a kind to brighten their hopes. If anything, the Barrister's pronouncements broke the basis of their fight into hopeless pieces and made thorough nonsense of their belief in a society that rested on propriety and order. Could their trial be that of a system? But then a system could not try itself. Suing for an amicable settlement would be caving in to evil. It would be watering the nursery planted with all kinds of demonic seeds and bringing them to full blossom.

"Barrister," Shechem said, "an amicable settlement is out of the question. We've done no wrong and we cannot seek freedom by aiding and abetting wrong. Let the matter be heard in court and if Dan Mowena so wishes he can convict us."

"We will be playing into the hands of a powerful syndicate."

"So be it!" Levi exclaimed with noticeable bravado. "Are we not in their hands already? Is Sanko not the dumping ground for their victims?"

"I admire your zeal, but let me say this, that others before you have tried and failed," Ekobena said, refusing to give up. "The hero's death you are inviting can be dispensed with. You know that the more stubborn you become the harder too will the reaction get."

"Steadfastness is not stubbornness, Barrister," Levi said. "We are holding on to a cause we believe to be right. Only give us your word that you will defend us in all honesty and strength."

"You have it," Ekobena said, then hurried to add: "but remember, money is the root cause of all evil."

10

On the day of the trial they were loaded onto a Renault lorry - Levi, Shechem and thirty other detainees whose hearings were scheduled for the same day. The lorry was yet unknown to people in Tole as it was only three days old in Sanko, having been sent there recently by the Justice Ministry to replace the Hino truck whose engine had knocked from negligence.

As Shechem wanted to refresh his eyes with scenes of normal life in Tole, he paid the five hundred francs tip to deserve a place by the side instead of being buried behind the rough-shaven skulls of other passengers. The prison gates released them quite early to enable them to arrive at the court in good time.

Eight months in Sanko had changed the face of Tole so drastically that he could not make out the streets and paths as they trundled on towards the court. Somehow the town had grown older and dirtier and the pace of activity seemed slower than he'd known it to be.

They drove into Edini gate with its line of bars and sawyer stands. The smoke rose as usual from the many fires on which the meat roasted, and the early hours notwithstanding, people milled about in search of things to satisfy their individual wants: men looking for women, women looking for money, bar tenders looking for customers, drinkers looking for alcohol. Shechem noticed that the place had lost much of its steam. There seemed to be fewer people about, fewer women especially, as compared to when he used to walk past headed for home from work and not responding to the inviting hisses from hang-about women eager for activity. The place looked somewhat neglected in spite of the apparent bustle, so that if it was a person one could say it was emaciated.

They left Edini gate into Kossala climb, but his mind refused to follow them. It remained behind, and went from bar to bar, from meat stand to meat stand; it roamed on the faces of the women, entered their heads and mingled with their yearnings and deceptions. It continued like that, rebellious in its freedom, until it caught up with a schoolgirl and her schoolbag, and a young, jobless degree holder who sat in one of the bars and watched her return home from school, day after day for three weeks.

He'd sat in that bar with no drink before him for he could not afford any. The bar-tender had threatened to throw him into the street if he continued to occupy space for nothing, and had only relented when he heard the percher's diction. The bar tender himself did not have only one but two degrees in his pocket. So he'd left the young man to his own devices and only watched with interest to see just why a well-educated young man would burn away his days in a bar staring into the street in sleepy idleness and only shaking to life when Benedict Tongley High School released its day-students into the street at the end of school. The young man had stopped visiting his bar during the holidays, and the next thing he had received from him had been an invitation to a wedding.

Kossala climb was a small mound of seawall that had been dumped for resurfacing work and abandoned to be compacted by feet and wheels into a permanent feature of Tole's road network. The town slab lay just off the climb. That was one place Shechem recognised distinctly. He had a fair knowledge of the volume of business going on there for having done a special paper on the meat trade in Tole. In its good time the slab handled fourteen slaughters daily. It also ran a cattle market which attracted buyers from as far off as Gabon.

Although they were driving past early in the morning when the sale and slaughter activity was supposed to be at its peak, he was baffled at the dry aspect of the place. The pens were empty and rundown and only a few scrawny dogs were to be seen sniffing the ground for the scant smell of blood. The clang of butchers' knives rising above the hubbub was gone. It was a dismal place they went past.

"Your house. See there," the detainee standing closest to Shechem said, nudging him hard on the shoulder and forcing his gaze towards his house. He hadn't wanted to look in that direction and was somewhat annoyed that someone he did not suspect knew him to the point of knowing his house was now forcing him to look at what he did not want to look at. He did not suspect the man standing by him would know his house because he looked at him and could not think of where on earth he'd ever met him. The only thing that gave away any hint of familiarity was the way the man kept stalking him on the lorry right from when they left the prison. He'd noticed, but without paying too much attention to it, that each time he moved deeper into the lorry the man fought his own way forward, step for step, space for space. Twice the man had smiled at him when their looks had met but he hadn't found any good reason to return the smiles of a man he had no business doing with and who besides was forcing his way into company he Shechem did not want to sustain.

The dust cloud was thick but not such as to shut out visibility completely. Besides, the mental picture he immediately summoned up brought the house into a relief which did not depend for its sharpness on the troubled visibility. The lawn was overgrown, just like the hedge, and the layer of dust on the roof was thicker. He noticed as they drove closer that one of the windows had lost a pane with its frame now being held open by a fat stone, no longer by the green metal latch.

His easy chair was tucked away behind that window. In the evenings, when the cold wind started blowing in, they used to close the window and turn on the radio or just sit together in the parlour conversing. Shortly before his arrest he had sat in that chair reading *Grace Notes*, with Kunsona by his side heckling him for mango juice which he knew he could only get by trekking half a kilometre into the centre of Tole. He'd closed the book mumbling to himself: "family symphony"; and the little girl had immediately switched her attention away from the mango juice to family symphony.

"What is family symphony, daddy?"

"You at least know what a family is, don't you?"

"You and me."

"But also your mother."

You, me, mother."

"Correct."

"And symphony? The word sounds nice."

"Music. It has to do with music."

"Can you play it to me?"

"It's not our own kind of music."

"What's our own kind called?"

"Nkwallah."

"Let me hear it."

"This is the wrong place for it."

A car, not the kind one could say was on its last legs, was parked some way off. It looked very much like a convertible metallic grey Mercedez 25O.

"Familiar car, surely," the detainee by Shechem said, nudging him again by the elbow and forcing his gaze in the direction of the car. A man was sitting in it with a woman whose features Shechem couldn't quite make out, but from the way the car was agitated it seemed they were engaged in a healthy brawl. The detainee by Shechem opened his mouth to say something but checked himself again, and until they reached their destination he avoided Shechem's eyes, dragging another detainee to the side immediately upon arrival and breaking into spirited reporting.

The courtyard was full, not least because news of the trial had suffused the town, but also because Motine Swaibu himself was enough event to fill any court hall. Shechem ran his eyes through the crowd hoping to catch sight of him for a quick check on his mood but failed. He was a man of pomp and ceremony and would not bury himself in the anonymity of a crowd if he could stand out and be seen and cheered or booed – he never minded the reaction so long as there was one. In fact he seemed to derive quite some pleasure in adversity, especially if it was of a kind to magnify his edge over his opponents.

It was even preposterous of Shechem to think for one minute that Motine Swaibu of all persons would reach the court premises before the culprits he was taking to the gallows. Weaker parties arrived first, never the stronger ones. In court trials, who arrived the premises first was psychologically relevant. Motine Swaibu was a fine partner at the psychological game and could be trusted upon not to miss the promise of pageantry and victory held in the looming encounter.

The detainees were left in the courtyard for some time under loose surveillance. They broke up into little groups of two and three according to affinity and strategy. Shechem searched out his friend who had kept to himself all through the journey from prison, and stood him against the eastern pink wall of the main court hall. The man's mood was downcast as Shechem could see, and he did not seem ready for any talking of whatever kind. But Shechem was. He hoped Levi had seen the way the strange detainee on the lorry had pushed his way into his private life, to the point of commanding him to see and take note of things he had set out to avoid, as if he had now become some robot that any detainee from God knows where could say look and he looked, don't look and he did not look. He wanted to discuss this whole thing with Levi. It was important. He searched for the detainee with his eyes and found him throwing his hands about in elaborate gestures and then holding his listener firmly by the shoulder to ensure that his words had been well understood.

"There," Shechem said, pointing discretely at the detainee. "Who on this earth is that one?"

"And of what striking importance is that to where we are?" Levi retorted, with a face that wished Shechem had busied himself with more relevant things.

"You didn't see him on the lorry, nudging me all over the place and forcing my eyes onto my house?"

"And I whose house never came into sight, what should I be saying? My dear young man, a severe prison term hangs over our heads. Think of that and stop fretting over a house and its inhabitants you may not be seeing in the next many …"

In the middle of this severe rebuke of one friend by another, a court clerk appeared on the raised veranda of the courtroom and ordered in a shrill voice that the detainees be marched off to the makeshift cell adjoining one of the chambers. They jostled into the tiny shed and were locked up. There wasn't enough space even for their feet, so they kept shifting and shoving in the vain hope that some magical extension would materialize from the blues. Shechem's secret hope was that the door would fly open any time soon and they would call Levi and himself out for the dock.

"Still too much noise inside here," a voice cried from near his left ear. He turned immediately only to find that it was the same detainee who'd kept prodding him on the lorry.

"And must you blow up my ear drums?" Shechem blew into the man's face. "Who on this bloody earth are you precisely?"

"What does it matter?" the detainee threw back at him. "But since you ask I'll tell you. Efuet Martin. The children called me Teacher Efuet."

"Teacher Efuet...Teacher Efuet," Shechem repeated, searching his memory for traces of the name. "Yes, yes! Teacher Efuet. The school fee scandal."

"That's it."

"It raised quite some dust in this town, I remember."

"Needless dust," the detainee said. "They said I ate the money but that's not true. I'm not the kind...now or ever. The HM. He used it to build his house, then sent two cows to Dan Mowena with the rest."

"This was two years ago," Shechem said in sympathy.

"Yes, two years, and I've been in Sanko since then awaiting trial."

This revelation by the Teacher lit the minds of the other detainees and each one opened a personal chapter of indignation.

"Me four years six months!"

"Three years I've been here!"

"Never tried, me. I've lost count!"

Someone banged the door from outside and demanded silence, that they would all be punished for any further contempt of court.

"What does it matter?" the Teacher cried, looking out to the receding figure of the clerk before crying out again: "Motine Swaibu!" as he pointed through the opening in the metal door.

Shechem pushed his way closer to the door and saw Motine in his ritual grey suit and black hat walking across the courtyard towards Dan Mowena's chambers.

"Back to your place," the Teacher ordered.

Just then the court clerk with the shrill voice appeared at the door and read out a list of six names, then said offhandedly, "These will be all for today," to renewed movement of protest as the lucky six made for the door in the process of being opened. They made up the famous Gang of Six known to rape and slay at random, and were just five days old in Sanko where Dan Mowena had offered them safe haven from a vendetta.

"Unacceptable!" Levi exclaimed, more in lament than in protest.

"Not if you cannot fight it," the Teacher said philosophically. "We will rein in our bitterness for now."

The cell fell silent as if the Teacher had also become the accepted Master. No-one knew where the authority came from, but it was accepted without question. Even Shechem who loved to command fell easefully under the spell of this detainee. The man's hold on him was such that he actually caught himself placing a finger on his lips to make sure he did not voice any disrespect for the call to silence.

Against the muted tin shed the courtyard buzz and bustle rose and fell like waves in a raging sea.

"You all know my own story," the detainee began when the silence had struck him as good, "why I'm here, how it was said, utterly maliciously, that I collected fees from children and swallowed same instead of paying them in to the HM." He paused as if to underline the enormity of the accusation. "My own case affects me alone and the children I taught, but there are others here whom we can term martyrs of justice."

A slight din rose and heads turned confusedly in the direction of Shechem and Levi, but almost immediately the detainee put out his hand and silence returned.

"You are right to search for them," the Teacher continued. "Shechem and Levi are in jail for the Truth. They uncovered the deeds of a bank robber in the guise of a Board Chairman. That's why they are here and not out there continuing the work they were doing so well. With them justice has been imprisoned."

The cell lit up and seemed to expand as if the walls were pushed backwards by invisible hands. Whereas it had been difficult to find room for the feet, it was now possible to sit and even stretch the legs. Most of the listeners descended to the floor and sat supporting their slanting bodies with hands planted on the ground. Only the Teacher, Levi and Shechem remained standing.

It was now that the detainee's features etched themselves out distinctly against the grey walls of the makeshift cell. He was a man in his mid-forties with a head that balded rather neatly, too neatly, really, for a primary school teacher. If he'd been a monk, that head would have sat beautifully on his shoulders. He was tall without being long, and two years in Sanko had not taken away from his vigour and fleshy mien. He had a rainy season voice, thick and oily, and when he spoke it travelled to you and enveloped you like a blanket. His mind and bearing were those of a sage, to which his comparatively young age only lent greater radiance.

"Justice is here with us," he pressed on. "If justice is in the cell, what is left in the courts?" he questioned in classroom fashion.

A listener put up his hand.

"Yes," the Teacher said.

"Injustice," the listener said.

"Injustice, yes…the thing and its negation cannot cohabit. Justice and injustice cannot share the same bed!"

"Teacher Efuet," Levi broke in, "this is a strong statement you've made."

"Strong…very strong statement," the listener who had put up his hand concurred. "If we have it here, justice I mean, then this is where freedom too belongs."

A chorus organised itself and before long the cell was one beaming song of freedom.

"We are free!"

"Freedom is here!"

"Free!"

"Free!"

"We are free!"

The court proceedings were brought to a sudden halt under the power of the song. Court officers emerged from business, together with their clients, to ensure that the hubbub was not prefatory to an uprising.

Teacher Efuet stood near the metal door stroking his half-bald head and looking outside, ready for any showdown. He was a man with a lot of fight in him, and if anything, detention had only strengthened his will.

Concocting a swindling charge and forcing it on Teacher Efuet like a scarlet crown had been the HM's genial way of resolving the seething rivalry between them. But as he came to discover, throwing his rival behind bars with the aid of a corrupt judiciary had only exposed him more in the eyes of the school and the public, especially after the initial dust had settled and hidden facts had begun to rear their accusing heads. The PTA had met in an extraordinary session and recommended that he too be relieved of his functions until such a time that it would become clear just what had happened to the children's school fees. The recommendation was still being examined by the school proprietor, but there was no doubt in anyone's mind that Teacher Efuet and the HM had swapped places.

"Justice! Justice!" Efuet cried, turning round to face the detainees whose faces all carried a serenity steeped in the pride he now incarnated. "We drag it on the ground or then bundle it in sackcloth and bury. Those ones from across the oceans who built these premises meant them to be the temples of Truth. We have turned them into marketplaces where we display the blackness of our ways! There! There!" he cried in the direction of the courtrooms. "What do they sit there doing, Dan Mowena and all of them? What are they paid to do?"

At this the listening detainees made a movement like the beginning of a stampede. "No! Not now, not yet!" Teacher Efuet cautioned as he caught the mounting irritation. "Their own justice has a face and a name. They will bring it down on us if we are not watchful. And we must be. Justice has only one bedfellow which none ever since the beginning of time has questioned. But we of this bad age have removed that bedfellow and put a bug in its place! See our consciences! The scabies! The sipping sores! The slime sticks and stinks! Where is the healing power of Justice? Have we ever but known it?"

Just then the cell door opened in a mad fracas and without warning they were emptied back onto the lorry, Teacher Efuet all the while crying in the direction of the whole court: "The healing power of Justice!"

As they trundled out of the court premises Shechem saw Bertha standing by a metallic grey Mercedes 250.

11

The detainees did not hear from the outside world again for another three months, until the day Ekobena came to tell Levi that he'd been admitted to bail. Justice Dan Mowena had seen to it himself and had commissioned the Barrister to "inform the other one in no unclear terms that his own release can wait."

Levi had turned down the terms as provokingly discriminatory and after a tirade on jurisprudence the Barrister had left to take the rebuff to His Lordship Justice Dan Mowena.

The emissary had been sent marching back with a series of punitive measures: immediate withdrawal of bail, sterner incarceration conditions, indefinite detention. For all His Lordship cared, and which was very much, "the two vandals can rot where they are!"

One of the consequences of Dan Mowena's anger was the curtailing of visits, and along with them the little privileges such as books and newspapers. These would otherwise have all been trivial privations but for the fact that they hit the deprived - Shechem especially - below the belt. Books, newspapers, letters, even people, one could replace with products of the mental factory. Their absence built the power of imagination into a new force that made men authors and editors, reporters and fashioners of human beings. Our creative scope soared with a brittle sense of omnipotence. Loss of freedom became indistinguishable from loss of sight as both resulted not in weakening but in strengthening, in concentration of surviving endowments. Milton, Wonder, Talla, these Great Masters shattered the stigma of rejection as their genius transformed their loss of sight into a salutary disablement. No sooner was Paradise lost than it was infinitely more richly regained through the resilience of the creative faculty.

All this stuff made perfect sense until the burning passion in you started tearing down the walls of your skin seeking release. The heart of a father seeking a daughter restored the mind to the reality of its weakness.

Day after day Shechem hungered for his daughter. Over and above the pains of confinement, not being able to see his daughter was the thought that afflicted him most. He lay awake through the night tossing and bobbing on his little bed, his head full of places he would have been in with her and the many irreplaceable things she would have been doing: the salt in place of sugar, the overflowing cup of hot coffee dancing in her hands, the midnight bang on the bedroom door because the monster was back in the dream again but really because she wanted to spend the rest of the night cuddled up in his arms with her mother expelled to the outer fringes of the parental bed…the hollowness now was excruciating.

He thought of Bertha too, but not with the same fondness. Which was strange, even to him. The court scene had done something to her picture in his mind, had warped it the way burning sun wrinkles a plastic object. He even tried to stand her picture uprightly in his head but the image kept falling and cutting weird shapes on the ground. He was no longer very sure who she was. The truth was he could no longer vow for her a hundred per cent as he would have done in the beginning years of their marriage. She seemed to have drifted too dangerously out of their marital orbit and by all indications it wouldn't be long before she became a stranger to it.

The court scene with her standing there by a metallic grey Mercedez 250 kept bobbing up in his mind. What message was she sending off in his direction with all that? He did not recognise the dress she wore as having been bought by him or with his money and her coiffure seemed to be sitting on a strange head, not on his wife's.

She'd been brought to the court that day by the hearing. So she knew he would be there. She had certainly seen him in conversation with Levi by the eastern pink wall of the court hall. Had stood by or sat in the comfort of the metallic grey bird and seen his skinny and ill-clad frame straining on futilities with his jail partner. She'd seen his pale frame and remained insensitive. By all indications, her soul of wife had been swallowed in the snare of the glittering limousine.

Who ever it was that owned the metallic grey thing was clearly a predator and once you slipped into the grips of such a man you were killed and devoured. No qualms.

At their arrest Motine Swaibu had been driving a 504 lift-back, but information had long since reached them in Sanko that he had changed to a shattering German high profile make. And it looked just like him. Anything that oiled his ego was welcome, even sleeping with his own daughter as it was rumoured he had done.

Shechem did not know how far he could depend on Bertha to fight off the rake's ruses which he was known to unleash in all kinds of unsuspecting ways. He boasted about that the woman who could withstand his advances had not yet been born, and then revealed as proof the names of his victims, some of whom were stunning in their familiarity and social position. He'd humiliated quite a few honest gentlemen in Tole and outside by simply tricking their wives into an affair and then noisily and ostentatiously dumping them to anguished pleas of please consider my status and that of my husband and why did you get me into all of this if this was how it was going to end?

The court scene troubled Shechem considerably. Knowing Motine for what he was, one could not put it past him to want to complete his affront by sleeping with Bertha. That was the way of all black-hearted men. Shechem wondered: Would his wife be equal to the task? Supposing her fidelity to him had been due to the absence of trial? Could she hold out? Did she have the resources in her to say no leave me alone because I love my husband and will not do anything to hurt him or my daughter? Was she the kind to spit in the face of an importunate intruder and say if I see you here again I will split your head with an axe and call in the police or burn your stupid face with boiling water? He was eager to know how she would react to a wad of banknotes held up enticingly to her face by a grinning Motine. What kind of thoughts would pass through her mind at such an instant? The glitter of jewellery and the flash of expensive clothes? Trips to America via shopping sprees in London? What would her mind respond to better? Motine's blood money or her daughter and her husband? He was eager to know, just as he was anxious to know whether she'd given Motine room to talk to her. I'm a rich man and you are the kind of woman for me and not for just any scallywag. Never mind that wretch who thought he could destroy me by saying silly things about me in a paper nobody reads. How did you ever find yourself in such hands? No no. I've always been looking for the chance to raise you out of dust. You are too much of a beautiful woman to be buried in dust with a little child and a failure who prefers prison to family. Had she listened to all of that? Actually sat down and given him space for all this scrap and then maybe nodded here and there and said she'd ended up with the husband she had because the idiot had pressurised her into marrying him even though she did not want it because she was expecting better offers and had really had some and just when she was examining them he'd shown up and acted in such hurry and despair she had no choice? What do you mean you had no choice? It was foolish of you to have listened to an adventurer who had no past behind him and very little future ahead of him. This is where your lack of good judgment has landed you. I'm sorry but where were people like you at that time to advise me? Now you are talking, my sweet little girl! It's better late than never. I've come with the advice and the way. Never mind. It's Motine Swaibu talking to you. I will make you a rich woman. Rich. Know what it means to be rich? And happy? Richer than those things that occupy my houses and call themselves my wives. I will throw all of them out and you shall be my only wife from now until death do us part. And who wants to die anyway? Not Motine Swaibu. I will marry you now, now, here. Oh how I long to marry you. And you? See... take..., it's all for you...money...money, houses. Where do you want us to go from here? Lagos? Dakar? Mombassa? Varsovie ? Varsovie. Do you know Varsovie ? You want to go there? And patati patata, only to turn her head. Hadn't it already been turned? Otherwise what was she doing standing by that hideous thing and looking so foolishly pleased with herself? And in front of Dan Mowena's den just for good measure? She didn't wave as they trundled past. Granted, she did not see him – is he sure she didn't? But that was beside the point. At least she *knew* he was being carried away in that lorry. Had she risen out of our dusty life into a world of tiles and chandeliers and silk and Chloe?

No objection whatsoever.

So long, though, as his blood was not contaminated, no mother-to-child transmission. The road to a deadly disease was always like that at the beginning, smooth and beautiful, with a lot of flowers bounding it and producing soporific scents that dulled your mind and made everything around you paradisiacal. And If Death Struck? Such a question never crossed your mind. Death? Strike? Who? Not me. A beautiful one like me? The road was smooth and sweet. You travelled it with alacrity; this companion today, that other one tomorrow. At times a travelling companion did not last a day by your side and you'd abandoned him for another one. The whole thing was exhilarating, intoxicating. But then you only fell once. And once you had fallen you could only gather dust or mud; in any case dirt. The world of chandeliers and banknotes was often steeped in glue of the stickiest kind, glue that swept you off your feet as soon as you stepped on it, and you fell never to rise again. Unless you were of the Motine or Mowena breed who no longer cared whether they were flat on their faces or on their backs, but who were certainly not on their feet because they had long since lost them to banknotes and chandeliers.

12

The Prison Superintendent declared an open day in Sanko, a holiday of sorts during which inmates could visit with other inmates and outside visitors were allowed more time with their imprisoned ones in the open yard. This was the first such day in their now close to one year in the place and the feverish joy it occasioned seemed to say something about the great expectations of those who had been cut off from the outside world.

Levi and Shechem were not expecting any visitors: in his learned wisdom garnered from seventeen years of infallible service to the law and from partnerships sublimated by an innate critical sense, The Right Chief Justice Dan Mowena, President of the Tole Magistrate Court, had judged it appropriate that the two detained journalists be isolated from kith and kin, so they walked across the yard into Teacher Efuet's end of the cell blocks. He was in Block D, the one that held people condemned for minor misdemeanours or still awaiting trial.

The cell was empty but for the transistor radio that spurted out muffled sounds from under the pillow where it was tucked. Levi extracted the device from its hideout and it immediately cleared up as if celebrating its own release from jail. The local station on which Teacher Efuet had left it announced news time and the visitors settled on the bed to listen amid the strange feeling of once more being connected to the outside world and its run of daily life.

The news opened with promotions and appointments in the Department of Justice and they listened anxiously for Dan Mowena's name, each one rehearsing his own wishes in his head. The Court President's poor record was public knowledge and one did not need to strain to imagine what awaited him. But they didn't have long to wait or speculate as his name was read in third place. He had been promoted to Magistrate Grade Three, up from Magistrate Grade Two, and confirmed as President of the Tole Magistrate Court with jurisdiction over three other neighbouring courts with no resident magistrate.

The appointments ended with a special release from the Minister of Justice saying something like a special commission was at work on the records of all senior magistrates.

Levi turned off the radio angrily but the news continued to reel on in Shechem's head, this time centred exclusively on Dan Mowena. He heard the man clinking champagne glasses with Motine and the motley come to congratulate him... Thank you! Thank you so much! The appointments have come and gone. You can see for yourselves. The wood of Justice has been shaken to its roots and only the toughest; no, what am I saying, only the most upright, yes, the most upright have remained standing because their feet are planted in the sustaining soil of Equity. And there aren't many of them. Eight. Only eight Magistrates in a staff force of more than seventy-six have been found to be worth their salt. Chin-chin-chin! To Your Lordship! Thank you! Thank you! He! he! he! The Law has eyes. It sees those who practice it with honour and dignity. The Scale of Justice. It weighs your every act and deed, and it is merciless in its sanction. Many are weeping and gnashing their teeth right now as a just reward for their breach of the Law. If you come to Equity with clean hands you will be raised in the eyes of the public. Only eight of us have been so honoured. Congratulations Your Lordship! Congratulations! To your health! Thank you! Thank you all very sincerely! I know there are some who would have rejoiced to see me disgraced. But Justice cannot allow such a thing to happen to me; not the Justice I serve with all my heart. And let those who seek my downfall know that life is a battlefield where the strong kill the weak. If they miss me I will not miss them! And I have the Law on my side. Bravo! Bravo!...

And Motine Swaibu jumping to his feet to deliver a toast to his friend on the occasion of his double distinction... I'm not given to lengthy words but when a man is justly rewarded there is no crime in saying so and saying so in many words. Dan Mowena has been confirmed and his powers extended. He is the second strongest Magistrate now after the President of the Supreme Court whose functions we know to be only ceremonial. There is only one Magistrate in this land now vested with real and broad powers: Dan Mowena! That's how I make friends. I don't consort with the insignificant. Idle slander-mongers have no place in my life... And turning to the man with bulging eyes sitting by him with raised head... he is my own type. And so we shall celebrate him. To Your Lordship! Chin!...chin!...chin! and chin! Chin!...

Teacher Efuet bumped into the cell almost as soon as Levi turned off the Justice Department ramble. He was panting heavily, as if he had covered a long distance in high speed.

"Yembina...I touched her out there in the yard!" he said excitedly, with no surprise at all at seeing his visitors. "I don't know whether to laugh or cry. Two years. This was my first time of feeling the body of a woman, my own woman. And that's all I could do."

"At least you touched," Levi said with envy.

"No! No! Horrible!" the Teacher cried in protest. "My whole body. What do I do with it now? I'm burning!" He was sweating slightly and his nostrils were twitching. Levi patted him mildly on the back but he still did not seem ready for consolation. "She was crying when she left me and I hid my face and cried too. Do these people know what they are doing to us?"

"All too well," Shechem said, "and they are enjoying it. Dan Mowena and his friend have deprived us even of the small pleasure of seeing."

"Shechem," the Teacher said in a sudden change of mood, "as I was out there in the yard with Yembina my mind kept coming back to you." He looked Shechem up and down before waving him to the bed, leaving Levi to his own devices. Levi forced himself into the invitation to sit down and perched at the foot-edge of the bed.

"The car…remember?"

"The car?" Shechem wondered.

"Yes. The one we saw on our way to court."

"Now I recall. The big one by my house."

"Yes, yes."

Shechem expected him to continue but only a sudden troubled silence greeted the wait. Teacher Efuet stoked the bald part of his head, then ran his spread right palm over it repeatedly before saying with noticeable difficulty: "He was not alone in it."

"Who, he?" Shechem questioned with annoyance and impatience.

"The man. Motine Swaibu."

"Teacher," Levi said emerging from his long silence, "we've visited long enough."

"That's true. Maybe you people ought to get back to your corner." This was said amid some signs of relief but which still carried streaks of worry in them. Shechem did not press the matter any further. However, instead of seeing them off or just standing where he was and waving them out of his cell he pushed aside the odd assortment of articles on the tiny cane table by his bed – comb, snuff box, chewing stick, jagged razor blade - and sat himself on the created space.

The afternoon was still young and one could tell from the rich noises in the yard that the open day was yielding rich emotional dividends.

"Have you ever asked yourselves how Dan Mowena could imprison me for two cows?" the Teacher queried with dramatic purpose.

"And why should he, really?" Levi asked. Dan Mowena was a permanent enigma to him and any episode or thing that could assist his understanding of the maverick was always welcome.

"And yet I was the last person he should have done such a thing to, normally; the very last person Dan Mowena would have hurt. Come to think of it: he and I were born same day, same maternity in

Camp Seven, the frontier settlement where our fathers worked, his as plantation labourer and mine as Headmaster of the Camp School. I was later to learn that we shared the same cot and only the arm labels, thank God! told the two women who their respective babies were.

"Dan's mother died four days after his delivery, so he and I grew up on my mother's milk. I still remember her laughing and saying how we used to hang on her tired breasts, each to his own, and would press and bite searching for scarce milk. My father for his part loved relating the vivid circumstances of Dan's naming. "You see the little boy," he would say often, "don't mind that he is today a teacher. He hasn't always been one. Shortly after his mother's death his father was moved to another camp, by which time he was strong enough to be weaned, so he took him along, but not without having asked me to name the child, an honour of a particular kind which I took very seriously. You don't come across such honours everyday, so I took it seriously enough to seek inspiration from Daniel 2: 19-28."

"Shechem will certainly know that part of the book," Levi interrupted. "He devours the bible as if he had spiritual bulimia."

"Not Daniel" Shechem protested. "Maccabees, yes, I would know, but not Daniel."

"Why bother?" Teacher Efuet said, reaching under his pillow for a bible. "Here," he pressed on, handing the book to Levi. "Read us the passages and don't give the impression that the bible is good food only for Shechem and not for you."

Levi declined the duty on the grounds that Teacher Efuet was a better reader and would put more life into the reading than he could ever do. The Teacher did not even wait for the explanation to run its course but opened to Daniel and shot out his hand to request silence.

After this Daniel went to Arioch, the commander appointed by the king to execute the wise men of Babylon. Daniel said to him, 'Do not execute the wise Men yet. Bring me to the king and I will interpret his dreams. At once Arioch took Daniel to the king and said, 'Here is a man found among the Judean Captives who says he can interpret the King's dream. The king asked Daniel, who had been named Beltheshazzar, 'Can you tell me what my dream was and what it means?

Teacher Efuet stopped the reading and then said in their direction: "My father here would moisten his right thumb which he pressed carefully against the fine Bible page and flipped it over, then would pull off his thick-rimmed reading-glasses and hold them firmly in his hand before turning to Mowena: 'you may say one name is as good as another, but that's not true. You need a name with a history. I will give this child a name that will accompany him through life and shine before him like a guiding star. If I hadn't already named my own son Martin I would have called him Daniel. Daniels have the gift of wisdom and foresight. You want a child like that, a child before whom kings fall prostrate in the manner of Nebuchadnezzar.' These were my father's words to Mowena. There was no evil in those words, as you can see. Dan Mowena grew up on my mother's milk; my father's deep faith in God provided him with the name he is so proud of today. But does he only remember the man who gave him the name?"

"And what leads men to such ingratitude?" Levi interjected. "Is it the primeval penchant for evil inherited from Eve? No amount of divine attention had deterred her, no extent of God's love. She'd gone straight ahead to league with the serpent and flout God's dire caution against the Tree of Life."

"Man's history since then has been a harrowing catalogue of evil repaying good, of injustice strangulating justice," Teacher Efuet said in agreement. "Eve sold her virginity off to the devil and brought prostitution into the world: prostitution of the flesh, of the mind, defilement, yes, defilement. In his Babylonian captivity the young Daniel refused to eat the unclean food set before him by King Nebuchadnezzar. The power to withstand evil, to say no to the serpent when it rears its ugly head either in the form of food or of the enticing flesh, that's what Eve betrayed, that's what Daniel upheld. My father named Mowena's son Daniel so that later in life he could say no and teach others to say no to the serpent in our midst. He has grown into the worst serpent himself, deadly in his sting, rounding up souls under his venomous coil." At this Teacher Efuet leapt from the stool and paced vigorously towards the door so that anyone passing would have felt the power of his invitation. Standing there by the door with half his body lit by the evening sun, and the other half in the cool shade of his cell, he held the Book open in his left hand and stuck out his right forefinger menacingly, then began to read, his neck tautly strained into the open pages.

"Seeing the crowds, Daniel Mowena went up to the bench. There he sat down and was joined by his admirers. Then he began to speak. This is what he taught them:

"'How happy are the self-righteous; theirs is the kingdom of heaven.

"'Happy the brutes; they shall have the earth for their heritage.

"'Happy those who persecute; they shall be hailed.

"'Happy those who hunger and thirst for what is evil; they shall be satisfied.

"'Happy the wicked; they shall have mercy shown them.

"'Happy the heartless; they shall see God.

"'Happy the warmongers; they shall be called sons of God.

"'Happy those who are celebrated in the cause of evil; theirs is the kingdom of heaven.

"'Happy are you when people praise you and adore you and glorify you on the devil's account. Rejoice and be glad for your reward will be great in heaven."

At the end of his performance Teacher Efuet threw the Book on the bed and it lay there bulged like an accordion in action. He did not utter any words again but stood, spent, looking at his two visitors by turns. Shechem for one was too charmed by the magnificence of the man's imagination to say anything. For anyone unfamiliar with the sermon, there was no hint that, far from reading, the Teacher had been re-making in a show of instantaneous outpouring totally reminiscent of the muses.

Even Levi took time to return from the biblical mount where the Teacher's sermon had conducted him. He robbed his face repeatedly as if trying to wake from a trance, then reached out and felt his friend just to be sure where he was. The mount had merged with Teacher Efuet's cell into one tangible reality in Levi's mind. The crowd, and Jesus in the middle handing down the new Law. Mathew the tax collector - also known as Levi - listening and storing everything in his mind, then later narrating it in the form of the Beatitudes, one of the most enduring of scriptural lessons. Levi the tax collector, then Mathew the apostle. One and the same person, but one born into the other. That salutary act of conversion that had changed Levi the tax collector into Mathew the apostle. Could something similar not happen to Dan Mowena? Dan Mowena sitting among the crowd on the mount and listening to Jesus deliver the sermon. And Jesus turning to him in particular and saying:

"But alas for you who have wealth, for you have been comforted. Alas for you who laugh now, for you will mourn and weep. Alas for you when the people speak well of you, for that is how the fathers of these people treated the false prophets." And hearing these words from the mouth of the Son of God, Dan Mowena abandons his old ways and turns to a new life of righteousness. This was possible. The word of God could enter the Justice's head and awaken him to the folly of his past deeds and throw him on the ground the way Saul was thrown on his way to Damascus, and then lift him up afterwards into a new being, completely transformed; lift him out of Dan the corrupt, Dan the boastful, Dan the crude, to a man capable of taming birds, of killing the thumping appetite for cows in him, of casting Motine Swaibu in jail, of freeing Teacher Efuet from bondage, a man capable of sitting on the bench and looking at both plaintiff and accused with the eyes of Justice and the Law.

The redeeming power of the word was infinite. Many bad ones had been rescued before Dan Mowena, made to feel the soothing grace contained in the Lord's preaching. Now was his chance. What did he see when he closed his eyes in supplication? For he was known to be prayerful. What land did his mind transport him to? What examples did he seek? Whenever he closed his eyes and clenched his palms over his forehead and whispered "Lord here I am thy sinful one," which sin did he have in mind? Corruption, false witnesses, wrongful condemnation, bad company, were these not the very sins that had built a home in his mind and made him prisoner to their dictates? He could yet break away from them, loosen their hold on his mind and come out free again like the biblical Daniel whose name he bore.

13

To Shechem, returning from Teacher Efuet's cell was like returning from a pilgrimage. What he'd just gone through filled him with spiritual nourishment of the kind that transformed Sanko - cells, grounds, warders, inmates - into a fresh new assemblage of purified sights and presences. Suddenly, every story, every inmate's account of himself, became different, multi-faced, variegated. Criminals were no longer criminals. It was no longer enough to say such and such a person had committed such and such a crime for that person to stand accused of the crime.

There were many Teacher Efuets in Sanko with similarly enthralling stories to tell, stories steeped in the redeeming sanction of biblical truth; many Teacher Efuets in Sanko with similarly enthralling stories to tell, stories shot through with the poisoned arrow of human greed.

Sanko was no longer a prison. Under the power of Teacher Efuet's scintillating memory, the place had metamorphosed into Auschwitz, into a concentration camp where the skeletons of injustice were gathered for burning… Babi Yar. Russia's own version of Auschwitz. The beginning of anti-Semitism is talk, is hatred - the end is Babi Yar: thirty-five thousand - men, women, children, shot and put down in a ravine to be buried; or then six million - men, women, children, cremated, incinerated, call it what you like, roasted, toasted, burnt. Killed, quite simply. Killed. Could Dan Mowena hear the cry of those victims? Could he smell the smell of smoke rising from the gas chambers? Where did he draw the line between Auschwitz and Sanko, between Babi Yar's cattle Jews and Teacher Efuet? Was there any line, really? If he could not hear the voices of Auschwitz and Babi Yar, could he at least hear ours? We who were closer to him? We whom he saw and touched everyday?

Babi Yar, Auschwitz, Sanko, Robben Island, Tcholire, Kirkuk, Mosul, places of deprivation, places of revelation. Man runs away from himself and goes round the corner and crashes into himself again. It's not me you imprison. It's yourself. It's not me you kill or starve or humiliate but yourself. Now that I see the extent of the atrocities, I feel thoroughly guilty. The Nazi war criminal who made this confession at the Nuremberg trials forgot that proactive guilt would have stopped the atrocities from happening, and that all this talk of guilt after the act was total bunkum.

Nuremberg tried white men for killing white people, many of them, millions: Jews from Germany and Poland and Russia; but also Germans and Polish and Russians who were not Jews. And the sight of what they did was ugly, uglier than Rwandan mothers throwing their children into the river to save them from slaughter. Volunteers picked up corpses from the street as one would pick strawberries in the front-house garden, and lay them on open carts, then bore them away and poured them into a mass grave where they knocked bones with other ones emptied there in truckloads.

At least there one understood the sustaining argument. Hitler wanted to clean up the Jewish mess and create room for Aryan purity. Such a rationale can be understood and even endorsed. It lies on the straight route to racial upgrading. There's so much trash around, all over the place. Millions of human shapes, the existence of which is thoroughly without meaning. The likes of these Hitler incinerated out of the way in his time. At least there one could understand. The chant of Aryan superiority rang in the ears with such beauty that one could not but succumb to its appeal. And Germans fell under its charm with the hysteria of voodoo faithfuls. Hitler had spoken. Hai Hitler! And the gas chambers churned non-stop, tirelessly, dutifully, to cleanse Germany first, then all of Europe hopefully, of man-shaped zoological impurities.

Tragic gullibility!

But theirs was not a totally blind faith in their Fuhrer. He had a dream for the German people. A leader who does not dream soon realises that he has no followers. Martin Luther King Jr dreamed; the Mahatma dreamed; Ken Sarawiwa dreamed; the serpent in the Bible sold a dream to Eve. Hitler had a dream for his people. They could see where he was taking them, and how. Death. Each death was a new beginning; each descending building room for a new edifice in the grand manner of the Aryan architectural dream. The Fuhrer was a man of great dreams, of great deeds.

But here, the killings, many, many. Countless. The genocide. What aim? What purification rite? A people are plunged into the cycle of violence that begets only itself. No help. No rest. No reward. Wasteland. The voices are crying in the wilderness. Howling…moaning…groaning. But the guns continue to break and to crackle; and the bullets continue to rain down, each drop a ritual of impalement.

We must keep vigil over the soul of the earth. Jesus did; Munira did. The day they picked Shechem up he'd just returned from his on Mount Bakingili, a terminal outcrop from an eruption on the giant Mount Fako. He'd spent the night there on a rock that still felt warm under his buttocks ten years after the activity; a night of watchful thought draped in low clouds. How does one keep vigil over the soul of the earth? The sins are many, so many the stars overhead pale in comparison. The cup tasted bitter to Jesus. It hasn't lost its bitterness. The world continues to be a very bitter place. But one must keep watch even in the thick of a malignant evil.

The black race complains of exploitation by the white race, but left to themselves black people devour one another like wolves in a herd of sheep and hurry to lay waste a land blessed with milk and plenty. The children flee, run, on foot and in wheel compartments of jets taking off for Europe: take-off without landing. The desert opens its dry mouth and swallows their weary legs bound for European dreams. The scanty survivors of the desert crossing drown their temerity in the frowning Mediterranean sea. Children flee from their land leaving behind mother, father, hunting dog; and some the little girl whose breasts they tickled in the dark. A whole life of promise raked by the greed and graft of a callous leadership.

Wherever one turns the story is the same. We don't steel: we loot. We don't kill: we massacre. We don't damage: we destroy. White people are not to blame for our station. Only idle fault-finders drag the white man into our dance of self destruction. It is not they who raise our hands and then bring them down on our own brothers; not they who sweep the banks and carry into tax havens in their country. Where can we go for justification of what we do to one another and to our land?

Slavery, colonisation, pacification: these inroads were made possible only by the rabid hands of African savagery. A cyclic and shifting savagery. It is now here, now there; but always it is somewhere on our land. There is no telling through which door it will jump in, or through which roof where the doors are held fast. Pitiful world, ours. Home to bleak forces. We have no hold on the powers of good; only the devil's grip on the forces of evil. Tenacious! Tenacious! The sun flies overhead, bearing its light to other continents, leaving us in the hands of darkness. At nightfall our genii come alive and remain on the rampage till dawn, refusing to go to sleep, refusing to take a rest. Thousands of years we have known the same turmoil. Of the spirit and in our flesh. The road ploughed is without relief: dry and hard, hard for the women, hard for the children, hard, hard for the men stooping with age.

Kings are kings to themselves only; and presidents too. The ephemeral kingdoms lie buried in the dust; the shanty republics totter on, draped in ridicule. See their children! See them in the desert, in the ocean, in the mid-seas; see their bones packed, stacked! No king speaks, no president cares. It's all fine. The children can die in the desert or sink in the Atlantic or the Mediterranean. No African king or president cares. If they speak, it's only to blame Europe for keeping unwanted niggers off their borders. But what are they themselves doing to keep their own wanted niggers within their African borders? What?

One man only we can present to the world with some redeeming smile: the Man-de-la. Man from there. From there, South Africa, country of the proud Zulu and the intrepid Inkatha. But country especially of the rational white man, Frederic de Klerk, type more than exception, who in the manner of great men stepped down and aside to give humanism a chance. Only a white man could have done what Frederic de Klerk did. No black man could have done that for his own brother. De Klerk did it for a black man.

It was not Mandela's courage that ended apartheid in South Africa. It was De Klerk's foresight and grandeur of mind.

The white race could have perpetrated apartheid for as long as they desired and nothing would have happened to them, except the burden of their own conscience; for they have one, unlike us. So they chose to give numbers a try and provide safeguards from the sidelines just so the country their genius had fathered did not revert to wasteland and bushland once again; just so the clean streets did not drown in rubbish; the neat walls in graffiti; the clean beaches in jetsam and flotsam; the banks in theft; the parks in carcasses; reason in nonsense; robust offspring in kwashiorkor; democracy in dictatorship; good management in chaos.

South Africa continues to be Africa's sole spot of hope not because of the ruling black majority but on account of the vigilant white minority whose cultural achievements black people all too often and all too naively mistake for theirs; theirs that will be found on proud display in the townships, in the DRC, in the Darfur region of the Sudan, in Somalia, in Rwanda, in Ethiopia, in Liberia, in Sierra Leone; in the minds and ways of each African who has not stopped to question why our history is so unremittingly black...so very bleak....

"Shechem! Schechem! What is this silence supposed to mean? Shechem! You're sleepwalking."

"Eh? Where are we?"

"Block D, on our way from Teacher Efuet."

"How did I get here?"

"With your two feet."

"And I did not crash into some wall or something? Frederic de Klerk, Mandela, did we discuss these men? The Darfur, Somalia, Sudan, what about these countries?"

"Neither one group nor the other. All along you have been one sullen block of moving object."

"I've just been experiencing a waking nightmare!"

"Were the names and places you've just mentioned those that crammed your nightmare?"

"Yes."

"But they seem to make sense even if I do not yet know how you came about them."

"They were actually the source of the nightmare."

"And what else did you want them to be?"

"What else did I want them to be?" Shechem reflected with slight amusement, then said to himself: "Just what they are not for the one, and what they are for the other. Why could the human race not collapse its fortunes into one uninterrupted sheath of shared experience? There were so many reasons why this ought to be so. Blood, air, the mountains and the seas, crying, laughter, pain: these gifts knew neither colour nor peoples. The peel of white laughter was no less contagious than the thunderous roar of the black man's laughter. If you locked a man in a dark room and administered pain so that he broke down and cried, you would not be able to detect from the sound of his pain whether he was black or white. It is true that the black man was on the whole more demonstrative in pain than the white man, but who had ever been under their skin to say that this difference was because the white man felt pain differently from the black man? And this little thing called the skull and the muddy stuff it carried called the brains. Why did nature or who ever was responsible for its being there not just give the thing the same power in each head? How could genius and blankness cohabit with such tragic facility?"

They had long since reached their cell and were now getting ready to join the other inmates in the refectory for a lean supper of plantain and weevils. The ratio of beans to weevils was about one to fifteen so rather than talk of weevilled beans the inmates talked of beaned weevils. It was easier to pick the beans out of the weevils than the other way round.

Shechem and Levi entered the refectory to a deafening din of spoons and plates and to confused chants of beans, not weevils! beans, not weevils! more plantains! more plantains! plantains! plantains!

In the midst of all this noise, the Chief Superintendent, Mbake Javis, was engaged in discussion with three of his Assistants in a corner just off the entrance to the kitchen. He didn't look the least bit ruffled by the uproar; in fact one would have thought, judging from the calm assurance with which he talked to the other three, that he was having a considerable kick out of the noisy protestation... Prison revolt is always a good indication of rigour and stringency and if well handled, always fetches the man on top a higher position and more pay. You cannot spend all your time dancing to the tune of criminals. Who ever told them they had a tune anyway? Sanko is not the place where you come to dry your wishes in the sun for all to see, admire and execute. It is the place where you come and eat weevils without counting them and smack your lips because the other option is starvation till death follows. It had happened a couple of times before and if the noisy rubbish does not cease we will consider the tougher line of action and see just how much they enjoy it…

Shechem waded through the noise towards his bench and dropped onto it without inquiring about how the protest built up. All around him the noise grew, louder and louder, what with the deaf ear given to their cry the inmates felt slighted and wanted to force attention out of the prison management. Some prisoners mounted the tables and stamped them hard and Shechem watched expecting the wood to give way under their feet and send them crashing to the ground. But nothing of the sort occurred. The tables seemed to have been built with such angry attacks in mind: thick wooden tops on bulky steel legs concreted firmly into the ground.

Shechem's body was calm inside, totally impervious to the teeming activity around him. It was just as if he had settled in a little world designed for him alone with peace and harmony as the only companions. The weevils and the beans, in whatever proportional mixture, the plantains and the clash of spoons and plates all looked like things of the netherworld on which his feet were planted as on the head of the snake of injustice.

He felt calm inside but it was a deceptive kind of calm. He managed to shut his ears and mind to the tumult about, but not to Levi's question, which had sought a niche in one corner of his head and settled there, making itself comfortable and turning the blood pumping in his veins into an angry surge of spleen seeking release. *And what else did you want them to be*? Indeed, what else did he want them to be outside what the people had turned them into? Wanting those places to be anything outside what they were would have meant jumping feet bound into facile optimism. Could the Darfur be anything but the Darfur? If you marched into territory like that with the flag of optimism, where would you plant it? On the wind-swept ruins? Who would hoist it? The eerie skulls littering the ruins? The vultures? You and your flag would constitute yourselves into a thoroughly risible spectacle, like these ones searching for good food on the plain backs of steel plates.

The commotion ceased abruptly, causing Shechem's head to ache inside and a new noise to storm his senses. When he raised his head he saw Mbake Javis standing in the middle aisle flanked by two of the three Assistants he'd been consulting with earlier.

Although it was late in the evening he was still in his Superintendents' uniform, a khaki outfit of safari design reminiscent of English colonial administrators. He looked quite grim in it, even foreboding. The inmates with the right sense of detection must have noticed that the man was in one of those moods out of which he never came without serious consequences to those who put him in it in the first place.

The spot in the middle aisle where he stood carried with it a rich tradition of solemnity that was solicited only very rarely and in the most grievous of circumstances. He'd stood there exactly two years ago – what a coincidence – to announce to the inmate population that Sanko was going to go from a mixed establishment to a male prison. Spoons and forks had sought his face in angry reprobation but he'd weathered the storm of their fleshly anger. The female inmates too had raised their voices from their own part of the refectory to add their disapproval to that of their male accomplices but Mbake Javis had stood his ground. Enough was enough. He was not going to be the Superintendent of a prison in which children got born without anyone knowing when or how they got conceived; where couples came to life without there being any traces of courtship; where men discussed sex as if they were all polygamists back in their homes and not prisoners meant to suffer the rigours of carnal deprivation. Enough was enough.

Even now the whole thing was besieging his mind again with towering vividness. The cardboard. The piece of plywood - he did not know which was which again. That shameful piece of wood behind which Sanko had transformed into one cesspool of fornication and illicit flesh trade, how did it get there? Who brought down the wall? Who?

"Who? Whhooooo?" His voice rang and echoed against the walls of the silent refectory and the inmates watched him perplexed. "The cardboard. That dirty shield. Who put it there? Don't answer but I sent the women away. They are all bringers of evil. With them here you could not do the penance you were locked up here to do. Prison is a place for repentance, where you remove your soul from your chest and put it on the floor before you and see all the nasty things you have done: knife, bullet, tongue, penis, all, and you say never again! But not you! You brought down the wall. Made fools of the Administration. We thought we were guarding repentant men but we did not know we were offering sanctuary to hardened fornicators!

"And today! The worm has climbed into your heads yet again and now you are drunk with the thought that through blackmail and riotous behaviour you can bring the prison administration into disrepute and why not obtain the shameful departure of its Superintendent. *A la guerre comme à la guerre!* Be warned: this is neither the first nor the second moment of trial of its kind and this one too will be crushed like those before it."

Something crossed his mind as if to caution him against open threats and he recalled one of the guiding lessons of penitentiary management: if you meet anger with open anger you only generate more anger, so take it easy while at the same time making the going tough for them. They should only see in your decisions that they have taken their protest too far. Nothing by way of threats should issue from your mouth.

"My dear friends, I have come so that we talk," he cooed.

"Not talk! No, not talk. Action! We want action!"

"We are ready to act, but let's first of all know what we should act on."

"The food! the food! small and bad!"

"Ok. Note has been taken. You want the food quality improved."

"Quality and quantity! No more weevils! No more weevils! Weevils, weevils!"

The two Assistants standing by him were busy jotting down what the rioters thought were notes but which were in actual fact the names of the ring-leaders. They had so far identified eight inmates whose role in the uproar they judged to be incendiary.

"Understood. From tomorrow you will notice a change in the quality and quantity of food you are served," the Superintendent assured from behind a mask of conciliation.

"Hurrah! Hurray! Long live Nine Lives!"

"Long live Stone Finger"

"Man Pass Man!"

"Victoria Tiger!"

"Long live all of them! Long live…!"

Nine Lives, Stone Finger, Man Pass Man, Victoria Tiger, these were the code names of some of the ring leaders. They had all been noted down by Mbake Javis's men, one of whom had kept looking at Shechem as if to say his silence was feigned as a cover up. In fact at one point a tremor had run through him when he saw this same one raise his head in his direction and then bend it again over the paper he held in his hand and scribble down something fitfully.

"I'll plead that you eat whatever is on offer today and wait for better things as from tomorrow," the Superintend said as he paced towards the main door.

"No!"

"Yes!"

"Ok!"

"But last time!"

"This should be the last time!"

"Tomorrow should come quick, quick!"

Not many of the jubilant inmates caught the grim look on Mbake Javis's face; not many of them either noticed that his steps changed into an angry march as soon as he stepped out of the door.

Shechem returned to his cell that evening with a heavy mind that told him the clouds were gathering over Sanko, black clouds that no sunrays could pierce.

14

The following day at supper eight inmates were reported missing. Their absence descended on the meal with more devastating effect than the weevils they had protested against and which the Superintendent had promised to remove from the beans. Everybody played listlessly with their cutlery: some tried to see how many rice grains they could lift, others how successfully they could grain all the prongs of their fork at the same time. The rice was the long-grained Chinese type - good quality, served with meat in cabbage sauce. The weevils were gone but somehow every heart yearned for their return. If this was the price to pay for their exit then the inmates were ready to have them back in any numbers they cared to return in, ready for any bean-weevil ratio that Sanko cared to inflict on them. But for heaven's sake they needed to know what had become of Nine Lives, Stone Finger, Man Pass Man, Victoria Tiger, Wikum, Mbah Atah, Ntonifor Alemkeng, and the grey-haired Ayuk Eba. They needed to know. If they did not know and did not care then the day they too disappeared into thin air no-one would care. Inmates could not just be vanishing as if removed by magic hands. Sanko was not the edge of a precipice where the least flutter of wind tipped people over and down below for always and their shouting voices receded into the depths of eternity.

The prison management maintained sealed lips over the missing inmates. No queries were answered, no explanations were offered. The silence grew more and more afflicting and the mounting sense of insecurity emptied the place of whatever residual pleasure being there had given the inmates. What macabre thing could Mbake Javis have planned and executed in so short a time and to such perfection? The chill was not in the number of inmates that had disappeared. It was in the kinds of detainees that had been targeted and actually taken away. You just didn't get up one morning and twirled Victoria Tiger or Stone Finger or Nine Lives or for that matter Man Pass Man around your little finger. If ten of you came ten of you were faced and overcome, any time, by any one of them. So what had happened? And who was next on the line? Who stood closest to the edge of the escarpment that Sanko had become?

The following day at supper they discovered that their weevils had returned, this time in swarms. There were whole armies of them in the pots and the captive beans jotted their besieged heads only very infrequently. The inmates ate with expectant delight, discovering a new relish in the weevils. Jaws chewed noisily and each inmate reached for more in happy and interested celebration of the return of the weevils.

Supper that evening climaxed with a song to weevils, composed instantaneously and taught to the refectory just as instantaneously. The composer and music master was Levi Mu'tum, who was known to be a chorister in the Bethel Baptist Church when he was not out in the field stalking news.

Weevils today
Weevils tomorrow
Weevils forever
Weevil is food
Bean seasoning
Weevils, not beans, feed
And fill
Starve not where weevils abound
Say never no to Weevils!
Never never no to weevils!

The refectory broke into song, a plea, a supplication. They had eaten the weevils. They had welcomed them back on their plates with joy. And here was a gay song to them in which the inmates expressed their love of weevils. They sang and looked at the door. Maybe the song would bring back their gone inmates; at least loosen the tight lips of the Superintendent and he would come and talk to them and tell them something that would soothe their hearts and put a glimmer in their minds.

They sang themselves hoarse, repeated the song over and over, now in high tones, then later like dirges. And then gently they streamed out, each one whispering the tune to himself and in a very special way to Mbake Javis.

Shechem's own whispering was attended by a new awareness of their collective weakness. These unexplained disappearances meant that the claws of evil poked out from the dark and danced over their heads ready to snatch them by the hair in the deep night and carry them to the meeting house where the barons of the night wined on human blood and dined on human flesh.

Levi kept up a silent pace, staring steadily into the courtyard light shot through by thick shafts of darkness. As they ambled along his steps became unsure, light, even airy, as if he was poised to fly not skywards but downwards, deep into the ground, into the dwelling place of devils. Suddenly, he stamped his feet heavily on the ground and broke into a run. He ran fast, faster, very fast, even much faster, as in an instant of flight out of and away from hell. He ran and hot air poured out of his mouth into the cold night. He kept up his effort, running, speeding. He was not running to but away from, even if every one of his strides seemed to bear him both away from and into. Watching him in flight, one could tell that he wanted to go far, far away from the claws that had reached out from the dark and dragged and pulled Man pass Man and Nine Lives and Stone Finger and Victoria Tiger and Wikum and Mbah Atah and Ntonifor Alembeng and the grey-haired Ayuk Eba and made them into no-names.

Shechem heard the orders pierce the night: stop or I open fire! Sto-o-o-o-p!

The voice became many voices. Shechem quickened his own pace, then broke into a scattered run behind Levi. At some distance from the main gate he heard a voice barking out orders: The gates! Man the gates! Pull them shut! Escape attempt! Don't let him get away! Open fire!

Shechem's feet could not carry him fast enough. The orders rang so fatally near yet remained so far away! His ears detached themselves from his head and sped ahead to catch the report of the gun. The sound came in one sudden bang, then rippled through the night like the clap of a furious thunder. All the running froze in his veins. That gun had surely beaten him to his friend's life, so what point was there running again? He walked, walked very slowly, the way a snail would do. And even so he thought he was walking still too fast. Where was he going to any way?

15

"He nearly succeeded," the tall warder said, blowing his gun, then went into convulsive laughter that lasted at least two minutes. In the piercing floodlight beams one could see the laughter as it peeled out and slapped their contorted faces.

Summoned by the snap report of the gun, the Superintendent had veered towards the scene. He broke a passage through the tight ranks and stood by the man with the smoking gun.

"He nearly escaped, Saa," the warder said again with renewed celebration. "If I had missed him Saa the night would have taken him from us."

"You did well," the Superintendent said curtly, more at the stars than to the man who had just shot Levi Mu'tum. "Dump him in the usual corner," he said as he turned to go, then added as an amusing after-thought, "this will teach them to jump jail." He withdrew without any further ceremony, his figure a thick block of authority and cold discipline.

"You!" the warder shouted, pointing at Shechem, "carry him and follow me," then started marching off into the darkness.

Shechem could not understand. Levi had not prepared him for this. In all their life together in Sanko, seeking freedom outside a just acquittal had never been contemplated. He did not know where in his friend's thinking to insert this act. It was all so sudden, so unexpected. Levi did not believe in chickening out. Otherwise he would have taken Dan Mowena's bail offer. But he did not do it. He said later when they had discharged Barrister Ekobena that accepting Mowena's offer would have been a cowardly act of betrayal. That was the Levi Shechem knew. This one in his arms, warm though bleeding profusely, was a strange Levi.

Shechem stamped the path mechanically, following the warder from a distance. He had not foreseen this conclusion. Many times he and Levi had talked of the day when they would leave Sanko back into Tole and start a Human Rights Movement that would check the abuses wrought by Motine Swaibu and his ilk. And now this. Where was the courage in it? How could Levi have run into a prison bullet just when the cloud was beginning to lift over their stay in the place? Levi Mu'tum...

Shechem remembered the day he arrived in the newspaper office. Proud young man with a stiff sense of purpose. Shechem received him at the chief's instructions and designed a profile for him. He remembered the young man's poorly ironed cotton shirt under a neatly knotted but creased marine-blue silk tie.

The mutual discovery hadn't taken place in the formal setting of the newspaper premises but over a break-time beer in *El Dorado*. First coincidence, they shared the same brew: Satzenbrau stout. With that common taste established, settling to conversation had been a pleasant formality for both of them. Second coincidence, the newly-arrived journalist liked *El Dorado*. He had struck a date there in the past with a young girl who later became his wife.

"You come to places like this to pick up free girls, not wives," Shechem remembered cautioning.

"Wives sprout best in suspicious joints," he remembered Levi arguing. "If a girl can love you in a bar, she will love you anywhere." Shechem had enjoyed the firmness of the proposition and the pronounced risk factor in it. A young man who shunned the conventional safe grounds for wives and instead staked his marital fortunes in the grimy putrefaction of a bar was certainly a unique phenomenon.

They had glided into the newcomer's recent past and his preparedness for the challenges of journalism. He had talked convincingly, and Shechem had been encouraged there and then to team up with him.

Working with Levi had been enormous fun, even if at times disagreements had come between them over some delicate ethical issues; like the one over Tendo's killing of the rapist sergeant, that had nearly ripped their tandem apart, and which Shechem recalled with a trembling mind. Shechem had argued in his editorial that two wrongs did not make a right, and especially that Tendo had been unjustified in hacking the spinal column of the rapist. To which Levi had retorted in his column that the editorialist was an even more macabre rapist than the man who actually carried out the act.

Shechem had smarted so badly under the assault that he had sued Levi before the newspaper litigation committee for character assassination and malice. The columnist had refused to withdraw his statement and the standoff had simmered on for three months, creating a divide between the editorialists and the columnists. The former had argued that rape, of however many women or girls or children, remained just what it was – rape - and was therefore not to be repaid with a higher crime. The latter had fired back that there was no higher crime than rape, and that in any event if anyone did not want to be murdered, he should leave people's wives and children alone, and that they would help in the killing of any rapist that was caught.

Somehow, the crisis had burnt itself out and gaps had been bridged over the irreconcilable passions. Otherwise, Shechem had enjoyed his partnership with Levi to the extent of endorsing his proposal that they take on the Motine Swaibu citadel that had landed them where they were now.

In spite of the heavy bleeding, the body still felt warm. The head continued to move, but not too loosely in his arms as he bore the body quietly behind the warder. A sensation of weight and weightlessness danced in those arms and trickled into his body and the bizarre jumble broke the track ahead of him into many small lines running towards the horizon. One of the lines seemed every bit like the road down which their two lives had come to be so entangled; a road smoothened by friendship and brotherhood, but also cratered in places by rivalry and misunderstanding.

"Move!" he heard the warder shout, then he discovered he'd been standing in one place with the drenched body in his arms.

"No time for tears," the man warned, stepping behind from where he could march him on more easily.

Shechem didn't even know he was crying.

"You people must be men of your acts," the warder said derisively. "One minute you are jumping jail and the next minute you are whimpering like a frightened baby. If he'd escaped do you know what would have happened to me? I would have replaced him in your cell the very next day. Move on!"

Move on. Move on. To where? To the offices of *The Chariot Inquirer* to announce their release? Or to Levi's house to throw him into his wife's waiting arms?

"Right. Turn right! Stop behaving like a stick!"

Shechem turned right into the brick-walled hut that until now he'd taken for a firewood shed or an incinerator of sorts because smoke was occasionally spotted over its roof. The warder stepped ahead and opened the door and ordered him in. When he lay Levi where the warder indicated and turned to go he thought he saw something that looked like a mound of teeth. The warder caught the movement of his eyes.

"You've not seen anything," he warned fretfully.

"Except what you brought me here to see," Shechem retorted, on the verge of anger.

"Which was nothing."

"Yes, nothing," Shechem repeated.

The pages of *Grace Notes* flooded his mind. In 1941 the Nazis made all the Jews of Kiev come together and they took them to Babi Yar and shot them. Evtushenko wrote a poem about it and Shostakovich put the poem into a symphony. Was this the kind of music his daughter wanted to hear? Music that celebrated the death of thirty-five thousand men, women and children. He could have played her a nkwallah. At least this one was a death song but not a pogrom song. Even so, would she understand? He could. That mound. How many teeth were there? How many rows? Sanko had once been a mixed prison where prisoners had got married and delivered children. What had the prison done with those children? That mound was part of the story, not all of it. What had the prison done with the children born in captivity?

Shechem stumbled back to his cell afflicted by the warder's statement of annihilation. NOTHING. The word rang with power in his head and gave meaning to his own life and Levi's death. There was no more frontier between his incarceration and the guilty freedom outside; between his life and his friend's death; between something and nothing. All was and remained NOTHING. But a nothing out of which something could be extracted with which to redeem life; after all, if his friend had turned down Mowena's conditional release it was so both of them could face injustice together to the end. He had died without saying why he chose that odd way out. That was no way to die. You died fighting, especially in a battle like the one they were in. You did not give victory to the enemy by running into his bullet and letting it snuff out the dream of justice just like that, bang!

He sat in his cell and clutched his head with his both hands as if to keep together the pieces it had just been blown into by an invisible gun stuck out of the night. He dragged and pulled his hair in a desire to feel the physical pain which the one in his heart was not enough to procure. His heart beat and cut quite alright in searing waves; he could feel his chest walls dancing like a cauldron of boiling palmoil under which the fire was being pushed and stoked incessantly. There was pain in there, in his heart, in his head, and now further down towards his belly. The thing was spreading with rampaging speed; soon his feet, right up to his toenails, would join in the symphony of torture.

It was difficult to say what caused him more pain: Levi's death or their own defeat in the war they were fighting. News would go out the following day that Levi Mu'tum had been shot while trying to jump jail. That would be the very first thing in the court premises as soon as business started. And then the papers would carry details of the escape attempt and the warder's heroic vigilance without which Sanko would have been dishonoured by a hardened jailbird. The thought of Levi's name appearing in the columns of *The Inquirer* put wounds in Shechem's heart for which there was no cure. Who would author such an article? Would the person bother to inquire into the facts of the accident? Or would he simply term it the predictable act of a hardened criminal and leave it at that? And if he did, what would be Shechem's own account of his friend's death? Would he simply content himself with saying that they sang a song to weevils and the next thing he heard was that his friend had fallen to the bullet of a warder at the foot of the main gate? Would such an account clear Levi's name in the eyes of the readers? He wanted to tell the world who Levi was and his deep conviction – even if there was nothing on which to base it – that the death was neither an act of cowardice nor one of betrayal. Maybe he should scribble his own version and smuggle it to the paper for publication. Or was he fretting over the whole incident for nothing? But what he was convinced of was that the court milieu would have a happy time showing how Levi and of course he himself were scoundrels being served their just reward.

The first thing he did the following morning was to rummage through Levi's papers for any information that would help clear the enigma of his untimely death. He had to do this and bolster his defence before the storm broke. He went through the papers carefully - handwritten bits, typed material, newspaper clippings: those papers surely carried the clue to Levi's end.

The collection contained an odd assortment of topics and genres - quite a discovery. Shechem had really never known Levi to be so richly versatile. His knowledge of his late friend's creative ability had until now been confined to the famous thirteen-act play they'd spent their leisure time reading, a kind of great and unique dramatic enterprise that summarized everything Levi had for the world in terms of products of the mind. The death of the dramatist now seemed to have thrown open a secret world of fiction and essays that illumined the complexity of his existence and philosophy, like this four-line piece titled *The Grave*:

I Love the grave
The eternal sleep
The final silence
Of muted walls.

The gloom of this short poem intensified Shechem's melancholy; but at the same time it provided him reason to believe that all along he'd been dealing with a mind resolute enough to place his pleasures distantly beyond worldly sanction. He now understood the urgency of Levi's journey through life and his messianic disregard for earthly trappings…

I am tired waiting for death, tired.
Tired waiting to see it, death
They talk about it

Fear it
But me
I long for it
I rejoice at the thought

God has prepared salvation
Let men enjoy it!
Now I am dead.
I can see the open hands of God's messengers
Welcoming me
First into reproach
Then into glory!

This one had no title. But the following two did and told in poetic beauty what it was about the world that pained his dead friend most.

The church bell calls
Yulina, attendant.
Go
Lay at heaven's gate
Earth's pains.

Tell God
I saw the child
Die
Hand open
For alms

He died
By the limousine
Gold-spangled owner
Inside
Buying

Knock at heaven's gate
Yulina
And inquire
Seek to know
Why Akotu died.

This one was titled *Sunday*. Symphony. Nkwallah. Songs of sorrow. Songs of pain. Songs of death. His daughter wanted him to play it to her. How would she understand?

The one below was titled *Barren Tree*.

Like gaunt hawks
They swoop
On the chics
Of technology

Like bursting vampires
They sit
Content
In their eerie mansions

Dungeons
Car-packed
Ports and strips
Adjoining

Nor fuselage
Nor plugs
Nor tyres
Their language can be

Yesterday they carried them
Across the water
Red
Of human blood

Today, here
They sit, apes
In their mansions
Redder with human blood

And so we raise a wail
And look
Behind the house
At the shamed shrine.

The last poem Shechem read was titled *Prayer*. He read it on his knees, as if in response to the piety of the composition:

The one thing that I knew was love
Love of all who walk this earth
My belief in this word was strong
And I lived only for this word

Then came the day when I saw in the world

Reality at work everywhere
My heart began to weep for the world
And my body sank low in gloom

All around there's a yearning sound
In my heart, in all the hearts
And the sky too is dark with rain
Won't be long till the storm breaks loose

Let's join our hands and bend down on knees
And search our hearts for all that is good
And give it force to overcome
And expel the evil in us!

The evil Levi wrote about was faceless, like the one that had killed him. The warder and his gun were just the visible arms of a sprawling force that rounded its victims up and crushed them without trace. That was the way evil worked and that's why it was so difficult to combat. Jesus had come and tried without much success. He'd fought counterfeiters, charlatans; he'd preached against sin in all its forms, but had died leaving evil in an even stronger poise than he'd met it. His death even seemed to have given the thing a new lease of life, comparable in power and beauty only to the pre-Arch days. When it meant to attack it did so with devastating force; when it was resolved to break human resistance it did so with thorough delight. Levi seemed to have understood this. That's why he was in such haste to seek the silence of the grave.

There were many other poems and essays Shechem intended to explore whenever he had the chance, but just as he was about to collect them into a bundle to string and stow away, his eyes fell on a paper. It carried Levi's tribute to Joe M. The paper had browned, like ember-shot smoke, but the writing was still quite legible. Shechem singled it from the bundle and threw the rest to the floor, then settled himself at a corner of the cell. His mind went back to the funeral, to the casket wrought in teak with gold handles, to the widow in black sitting by it with her two daughters by her in frilled white gowns, to the rich gathering. He saw Levi rise to the lectern and the gathering fall silent. He started reading, but the voice he heard was not his but instead Levi's. It was strong, cadenced, appealing. 'There are times in life we question the very sanity of our earthly presence. This is one such time. We plan, forecast, caress hopes and dreams; then bang, and all is brought to naught. We quarrel and fight, hate and spite; then bang, and we are stuck with the foolishness of our hatred and spite. What a joke: our earthly existence.

'There are times in life we listen and hear nothing, look and see nothing, reach out and touch nothing, ask and have nothing. This is one such time. Listen as we might, we will never hear him again; look as we might, we will never see him again; reach out as we might, we will never touch him again; ask as we might, he will never answer us again. He is gone, blown out, like a candle in the wind. Terrifying, yet so majestically real. Here it is, here, before us. This is all we are left with: a weird gift of flesh and bones, lumped in a casket. And even that, too, soon, we shall not have. All shall only be nothingness, and the terrifying interrogation: was the parting smooth? Did we do enough? Is there anything we should have done that we did not do? Some love we should have shown that we held back? Some care we should have lavished that we did not? Some friendship we should have sowed that we did not? Did we do enough? If we failed in any of these things, it's too late; but there is yet a lesson there. Every death is a new chance for the living; every end a fresh beginning for the quick.

Joe M. drove into the embrace of his destiny on Sunday 6 August in the afternoon. Road accidents are second in their unpredictability only to death; death whose fatal messengers they are, alas!

He did not die alone. His wife accompanied him and - oh cruel thought - so did a two-month old thing, crushed out of all recognition, her innocence notwithstanding. Under such circumstances, are words any use? If we talk it's just because we have the breath in us to do so; if we mourn, it's just because we have the sadness in our hearts to express; if we protest, it's just because our human frailty prompts us to it. This kind of end also ends all things, good or bad, for it reminds us once again, and in the most tragic manner, that we are masters of nothing on this earth. So what do I say to you, my dear friend, indefatigable worker in life's vineyard? What do I say to you? What do I say that you do not know already, now that you are in the realm of the all-knowing and all-seeing? Nothing, if not that we shall learn from you to live everyday on this earth as if it was our last day. For who knows for whom the next bell tolls? Yesterday it was for you; tomorrow it may be for me. Who knows?

Thank you for the lesson

Levi Mu'tum

Shechem put the paper away. It was only now that he noticed that his chest was soaked with tears from his own eyes.

16

Shechem's wife was a little woman with a strident voice. If you only heard her and did not see her you would imagine a heavy mass of flesh plunked in one corner of a jammed room and causing people to fly into each other with bullets of contradictory orders. But her physical sight changed all that. She was small, almost fragile... just the kind of woman who caught your looks and kept them.

It was difficult to say what part nature and the circumstances of life played in her being talkative. But talkative she was, for sure. She talked a lot, and her family conditions gave her more than enough material for her indulgence. Their daughter's ufos, his own silences, a leaking roof, unwarranted visits, these were all fuel for her vocal engine. She talked into the kitchen, talked out of it; talked while asleep. If God had been a married man, one would have thought He fashioned her on a day of a spectacular fall-out with His wife. But we knew the Creation to have been conducted in divine solitariness, somewhere in the deep void of pre-existence. Bertha was thus a unique woman talented with the power to talk, and making full use of it.

His arrest and imprisonment seemed to have dried up quite a good part of that buoyancy. During the first days of that arrest she closed herself up and spent long hours roaming her watery eyes on objects and people with no exact idea of what she was after. Her nights too became early and silent, the nights of a woman running away from daylight and its trials. Once she locked the doors and turned off the lights, she clutched her daughter to her chest and then spent the rest of the night listening to her breathe and at times repeat her ufo games.

It was on one such night, barely three days after her husband's arrest, that Motine Swaibu came calling. Kunsona received him at the door, then ran to the bedroom to announce to her mother that a certain daddy had arrived, before wondering to herself why this daddy and not hers.

Bertha emerged from the room catching her falling wrapper with one hand and smoothing her sleep-filled eyes with the other, with no time at all to fault her daughter for letting a man – any man - into their home at such an hour. She didn't even know who she was coming out to meet, and she least expected the man she saw.

The first thing that greeted her as she emerged from the room was the choking odour of lavender, the virulent kind used by charlatans in

Indian magic incantations. Out of politeness she kept her nose free, even though she felt an inner urge to block the odour from assailing it.

The lavender smell suffused the entire room, transforming it into a magic den with Motine Swaibu as the magician-in-chief. He hadn't waited to be given a seat but had chosen one himself, Shechem's leather rocking chair, into which he'd allowed his considerably fat body to settle. One thing the visitor had going for him was his innate sense of drama. He could in just one tactical turn score many significant victories. Settling in that rocking chair was one such turn. It was nothing short of full possession, not only of the house owner's authority, but also of the material and emotional prerogatives that went with it.

It took Bertha time to notice that the visitor had in fact settled into her husband's relaxation chair. And when she looked at him she found a man completely at peace with himself, even victorious under the skin. The mixture of surprise and indignation made speech difficult, so that she just sat staring at him, her drooping chin held up by her left palm. Her daughter sat by her in a posture of filial mimetism. No one spoke, even though everyone was speaking inside themselves. It was Bertha who broke the silence.

"You are in Shechem Nu'mvi's house," she said in his direction, all too aware that she was saying the obvious, but hoping that it'd send him away fast so that she could slam her door shut and lock herself back up again in her loneliness.

"I know," he answered, with studied calm.

"What then can my daughter and I do for you?"

"Nothing," he answered dryly.

"So why are you here?"

"Just to visit. I've been coming here for the past three days but have not wanted to enter the house. Even now I'll not be long." These last words caught him on his feet already, his right hand buried in the voluminous gandoura flowing over his expansive body. He cupped his left hand in invitation at Kunsona who instead buried her head under her mother's armpit. "Never mind," he said, as he dropped a thick envelope on the stool in front of him. "That's for you."

"Thank you very much, but I'm not sure we need it," Bertha said, without any emphasis.

"One never knows," he said, and then made for the door and walked out into the dark night.

Kunsona watched him leave, then collected some cool water from the fridge, gurgled it noisily, spat the mouthful on the floor, took a strategic seat opposite her mother, and planted her stern eyes on her.

Bertha kept her eyes on the white envelope on the stool where the visitor had dropped it. Something said she should just ignore it and return to sleep, but she listened to the stronger, more insistent inner voice that ordered her to remain where she was and not remove her eyes from the object.

The white envelope soon disappeared from view and in its place now stood a huge mound of white shapes, all dancing and shifting and re-casting themselves into new and more lurid shapes, moving yet standing still, now flat, now soaring to captivating heights. Castles formed, ships and cars, cars of rare magnificence. Bertha reached out her hand to touch one of the cars that attracted her specially and then discovered that her hand instead hung in the air. But the car was moving, disappearing in bends and appearing again at other bends.

She left the car alone and concentrated instead on one of the castles that had now transformed into a gabled brick house with wide glass windows and lush yellow blinds fluttering in the agitated wind. She marvelled at the splendour of the edifice, at the spotless glasses, the pleated yellow blinds, the sleek walls, the woodwork visible just behind the blinds. Her head started to reel, to go round in fast circles, swooping and thumping. She tried to steady herself but a great force seemed to be in control, a great force over which she had no influence.

Her head reeled, then steadied a bit. And the house with gables shot out from the cloudy background and slumbered forward, almost falling out of its eerie setting. Bertha threw out both hands to stop the house from falling, but discovered that there was nothing for her to stop or even touch. But the house was so attractive! Shechem hadn't promised her such a house. She did not remember hearing him describe their family home to her once they were married.

He hadn't made any promise or described any house to her. All he'd spent time telling her in the few months before their wedding was that both of them were to jump into the world like builders in a wide field. No house, no car, no promise, only talk of hard work and effort, sweat and suffering. And with all that she'd still clung to the marriage plan and they'd gone ahead to become husband and wife amid prognostications of ineluctable crash.

The talk of failure did not trouble her at all. Everyone was free to say what they liked about her marriage; she alone had the key to the union. People could say this or that rubbish about her life with Schechem; no one knew that their affection for each other was strong enough to weather even the most violent storm.

But what she was in this evening was more than a storm. A storm could break and subside with little or no damage in its wake. Her marriage life was a testing ground for such moments. She could not count the number of times a crisis had whacked her and Shechem and left each of them feeling that they'd reached the end of the road, and then miraculously the turmoil had gone away again leaving their union stronger than it had met it. Storms were like that: unpredictable, at times even beneficial.

The white mound was growing in volume, swelling into something almost monstrous. The gabled house started to crease and crack. The bends in the roads disappeared so that the cars flew into an abyss and never came back up again. A gigantic smoke started to engulf the mound. First it ate up the crackled house, then rounded up all the bends and swallowed them up before beginning to dance towards Bertha. She began to scream. Her daughter rose and seized her by the hand. Bertha raised her to her laps and bent over her protectively, her eyes still fixed on the white envelope where it lay, just as white, just as bulgy. Her chest thumped and contorted against Kunsona's young side, dragging the little girl more resolutely into the waking nightmare.

Kunsona looked at her mother in the face, then queried: "Mummy, is it the envelope? "

"Yes, my dear child."

"Then leave it alone, mummy."

"I don't know. The truth is that I don't want to touch it."

"What is in it, mummy?"

"Money, my daughter, money."

Her daughter's face darkened. "Will you touch the envelope then?"

Bertha did not answer. A worrying look clouded her face but her daughter did not see it since her own eyes were all fixed on the white envelope. Since her husband's arrest, money had stopped coming in, but the problems had not dried up in the same order; they stormed in instead, as if chased from the streets by a whirlwind. Admiring other women in their fashion displays had now become a favourite pastime. She saw items she found attractive, dresses she would have loved to put herself in, hairstyles she wanted to adorn, but the money for these things remained elusive. She did not mind the deprivation, though, especially since it was for her husband's sake; but she wanted to be able to know when it would end. She could not continue like this, not knowing for how much longer the trial would persist. The material hardship was worsened by lack of emotional fulfilment. Everyday she went to bed alone, spent the night alone, rose alone, went through the day alone. Quite often she longed for a man's warm hands around her, longed for a man's tickling words in her ears, longed for a man's powerful grip in bed. Or was she asking too much? Ever since her husband's detention, none of his friends had come to see how she and Kunsona were faring. It is true he did not keep many friends. In fact, outside Levi with whom he was detained, Bertha did not know of any other man in Tole whom she could term her husband's friend. But even his colleagues could have come round to check on her, at least give her some reason to feel part of a larger human community. Only Motine came, bringing with him a mound of interrogations. How was she to relate to this man who threw her husband in jail and then came to visit her in the night? Was the answer in that white envelope? Could the content of that envelope be the key to the enigma? He'd made straight for her husband's leather rocking chair in a defiant act of possessive substitution. And she'd allowed him to occupy that seat. Why hadn't she tipped him over, knowing how wicked he'd been to her husband? Why hadn't she shown him the door immediately and flung his white envelope after him in dual rejection? What moral sense was there in opening your house to the very man who'd brought so much sorrow in your life? But then, what sense was there after all in much of what we did in life?

"I will touch it," Bertha said in a half whisper.

"What, mummy, what?" the little girl queried, jumping down from her mother's laps.

"The envelope."

"Will you, mummy?"

"Yes," Bertha responded as she rose and collected the bulging white envelope from the stool. Between the living-room and her bedroom the envelope fell from her hand three times and each time she bent and picked it up.

The next time the visitor came, Kunsona's mother showed her to the children's room and not to the parents' bedroom where both of them had slept since her father's arrest and detention.

The children's room was mouldy and lonely, and unusual noises from her father's bedroom murdered the little girl's sleep all night.

Bertha was growing more and more fond of her nightly visitor. Each time he came she felt reborn, reinvested with a new strength and relevance. The money he gave her, the regularity with which he did so, this particular design of his worked favourably on her mind and body, so that as the days ground by it also became easier for her to etch a smile each time his image flashed through her mind. The only shade of darkness came from the distance Kunsona continued to keep from him, which biscuits and kind words had so far failed to absorb. But this did not trouble her that much. Time would take care of that, she was sure. Already, Kunsona was beginning to answer his greetings, even if only very gruffly, but at least that was already something to hang on to. With time...with time. With children you just needed to be patient and persistent; they always ended up doing your bidding.

The place her dealings with Motine Swaibu had taken her was quite difficult to locate. It didn't present any clear contours the way a love or a friendly relationship did. It was shifting, elusive, almost impossible to grasp. One day she went to bed thinking she loved him; another day she went to bed feeling only a slight sense of indebtedness to him; another day still she went about her business in the mood of a woman brought to fulfillment by a man's money and affection. She did not know, she could not tell. On at least one occasion she'd made up her mind not to open if he knocked, but then had caught herself rushing to open as soon as she heard a knock on the door. Once she'd kept him up past midnight, hoping faintly that he'd rise and leave, but also wishing that he didn't; and at the end when he'd asked to be led to the bedroom she'd done so with feigned sluggishness.

The wordless confidence in his conduct made it difficult for her to put her finger on the nature of their relationship. He talked very little. No expression of sentiments. Only his money spoke, strongly, loudly, visibly, and persuasively as things were showing. He gave it in large sums, regularly, never waiting to be asked. He knew that money had power and the best force of conviction.

His visits had become nightly, and there was hardly any night he visited and went away without leaving an envelope on the bedside stand. It had become a ritual which he performed with religious fidelity, and the two acts had woven with time into one in the woman's scheme of things, so that she could no longer tell whether it was his visits or the money they procured that she cherished most. But the entanglement notwithstanding, she still felt inhabited by a mood that would not be there if all the arguments were only materialistic. That mood had become strong enough of late to justify certain acts with a tinge of fatalism, such as what she did on the day of the court ruling.

Bertha had actually allowed Motine Swaibu into her marital room, where she'd surrendered herself into his arms, and wriggled to his caresses. Above all, she'd allowed him authority over her body. This was no discovery. It was a decision, taken with the independence of good judgment. No-one had forced her into it. Nothing, either. She was responsible for that decision in a way so thorough as to render any questioning, any polemics, futile.

But what she was not sure of now, what she could not say for certain, was whether that authority had scraped anywhere close to her heart. Even if it had, which she was not very sure about, what she knew was that it had not made any dents in it.

The whole thing was so confusing; yet there was some part of her that thought it was more exciting than confusing. But whatever it was, the deeper it grew, the greater the kick she seemed to get out of it. For one thing, the ambiguity she placed herself in led to the discovery of vast chips in the way she steered her life. Here she was, for instance, allowing herself to dance to new tunes, away from the stereotypes of a predictable, charted order. She discovered that she was no timepiece, but a web of active matter that could be both chaotic and spectacular in their ways.

She no longer knew where she stood between Motine Swaibu and her husband. By all indications the picture of the latter had receded to a pallid corner in her mind. It was no longer the luminescent presence that flooded her whole body with sweat at the mere thought of it. These days she pronounced her husband's name less and less frequently, and invented all kinds of reasons not to visit him in detention. Whenever she received any words he managed to scribble to her, a sense of indifference, even irritation, hovered over the thing as she read it, more out of compunction than pleasure. A thought even started germinating in her mind: and what if he never returned at all? How would that be? She thought such an idea would send her screaming, but she was surprised it didn't. In fact she turned the likelihood over and over in her mind and was quite amused that at no point did her conscience flay it. What not long ago would have been a horrendous thing to contemplate now sounded tolerable, even attractive. If she'd spent this length of time without him, she could stay for even longer; after all, what was it she missed in him? Material comfort? Love? Respect? His own brand of love, maybe. But then the love he had for her was not unique. Motine Swaibu had proven to her that love could always be substituted, sublimated, that love gathered more force when it came riding on the crest of affluence.

With all these contradictions besieging her mind, the prospect of the trial began to lose its attractiveness of freedom and reunion. Even the chances of him regaining his freedom immediately were quite small, if Motine Swaibu's contentions were anything to go by. The last time he had visited, which was just one day ago, he'd reassured her that he'd put everything into the case "to keep the wretch in Sanko until no hair was left on his head". With a statement like that coming from such a man, Shechem's fate was as good as sealed. Motine Swaibu knew that his tandem with Dan Mowena was impregnable in its power to bend situations. When money was put at the service of the law, made to blind the eyes of justice, used to blunt the retributive sting of the law, the likes of Shechem did not walk away from Sanko free. All these things Motine Swaibu had said to Bertha on his last visit, and had said them with enough confidence to give them a smack of finality.

17

They were unusually quiet on this trip, very unlike Sanko detainees. Teacher Efuet for one sat at the edge of the truck with his right hand dangling out wearily. His head, the baldness given sharper luminosity by the sunrays that bounded off it, was stationed close to a plank railing.

They were heading to court, most of them in the hope that their matter would come up for hearing and they would know whether they were prisoners or free men; but quite a few of them too with no illusion about their own fate. Shechem belonged to the latter category of detainees, His Lordship Justice Dan Mowena having decided that his matter would enjoy indefinite adjournment.

What he could not explain, though, was why he'd been called among the detainees to travel to court that day. He'd smuggled an appeal letter to the President of the Supreme Court quite alright, but nothing had come back to say whether the letter had reached its high destination or for that matter whether its strongly pathetic style had had any effect on the man.

The rough and tumble of the lorry settled him into a sub-conscious rhythm that blotted out the journey, replacing it instead with readings from the book of Maccabees...*Her temple has become like a dishonoured man, the precious objects that were her glory have been carried off as booty, her babies have been murdered in the squares, and her young men killed by the sword of the enemy. What nation has not received part of her treasures and taken possession of her spoils? She has been stripped of all her adornments and from the freedom that was hers, she has gone into slavery. Our beautiful sanctuary that was our pride has been laid waste and profaned by pagans. What is there to live for?*

He didn't come out of his reverie. He only steadied his mental button on the big question the book of Maccabees asked him: what is there to live for? Down life's road paved with graft, murder and lust, what indeed was there to live for? Mattathias, son of Simon, had cried out in protest: *Alas! Was I born just to witness the ruin of my people and the destruction of the holy city? Shall I sit by while she is in the hands of her enemies and her sanctuary in the power of foreigners?*

Shechem planted his feet firmly on the elusive floor of the lorry and opened out his hands. It was an unusual posture for a detainee travelling to sure conviction, but he took it. The other passengers looked up at him, Teacher Efuet most keenly.

"I will not let it happen," Shechem bellowed. Even without knowing what occasioned the threat, some passengers rang out in their turn: "No! no!"

"No!" he proceeded, strengthened by the chorus of protestation that had greeted his first pronouncement. "Like Antiochus Epiphanes I will make him sing out: *Now I remember the evils I did in Jerusalem, the vessels of gold and silver that I stole, the inhabitants of Judea I ordered to be killed for no reason at all. I now know that because of this, these misfortunes have come upon me and I am dying of grief in a strange land.*"

Teacher Efuet jumped to his feet and almost fell out of the lorry, so high was his performance. "Listen to him. Listen carefully. This is the voice of reason that speaks. Sin shall be repaid for sin, crime for crime, injustice for injustice! I say this particularly in what concerns Dan Mowena."

"My invocations are on Motine Swaibu," Shechem cut in. "The noose is tightening. Something tells me it is."

"The noose of justice never loosens," Teacher Efuet trumpeted, and the rest of the passengers chorused after him: "Never! Never!"

The lorry sped on, then swerved out of sight, swallowed both by dust and the deep bend in the road.

18

The court on this day was a monastery; a cemetery, even. Figures, all of them unfamiliar, moved up and down in silent rumination, their black cloaks and cream wigs adding more piquancy to the weirdness. The big tree behind the registry carried hundreds of black sparrows, but none of them chirped, or even fluttered, not even with the slight wind about. Weighed down in this way by its silent visitors, the big tree cast its mute shadow over the registry, enriching the attendant weirdness further.

Even Justice Mowena's chambers was lifeless, and this at a time when, normally, it would be engrossed in a rich buzz and hum. Mowena would long have been seated behind his file-stacked desk, re-ordering the case files in descending order of monetary importance, then ringing his secretary in for practical instructions on how to position the day's clients. But in the heart of what should have been a busy day, his office was still locked, with blinds pulled.

A clerk showed the lorry to a corner not far away from the main court hall, and ordered the detainees to remain onboard until they were identified and asked to climb down; an exercise he did not stay on for, but turned away stiffly and disappeared into a little office also caught in the brooding shadow of the big tree.

As instructed, none of the passengers left the lorry. They all remained onboard and watched the court scene from openings in the sides of the vehicle, eyes directed as if by agreement at Mowena's office, scrutinizing the fastly-held door for clues to his whereabouts, and the door staring back at them with even deeper surprise.

The same clerk emerged again from his little office with a piece of paper flapping desultorily in his left hand.

"Nu'mvi! Shechem Nu'mvi!" he ordered in a shrill voice.

Shechem shot out his hand with a start.

"Down! Get down!" the clerk ordered, whipping the air with his right hand. Shechem foraged his way through to the edge of the lorry, but not without first of all pressing Teacher Efuet's hand in his. As soon as his feet touched the court grounds, the clerk ordered the driver with a whisk of the hand to take the rest of his passengers back to Sanko, at which the lorry immediately roared to a start, scattering the silence into thick pieces that one could see flying here and there.

"Follow me," the clerk ordered, then took the lead in gestapo steps. Some way off his little office he stopped, turned round, and seeing that Shechem was following dutifully, turned again and marched on.

"Go in," the clerk ordered, as he stepped aside to show Shechem into the little office. He stepped inside and into the presence of a man in a black gown and grey wig, sitting behind a table as tiny as the room itself was small.

"Shechem Nu'mvi, I imagine," the man said.

"Yes," Shechem answered curtly, still wondering where exactly he was and what he was doing there.

"Pull that chair and sit down," the man said, pointing to a chair in a corner.

Shechem did as he was told.

"Do you know Motine Swaibu?" the man asked with urgent directness.

"Yes, yes," Shechem replied, and was about to add some more things when he was stopped by the man's raised left hand. His right hand was busy taking notes.

"How long have you been in detention?"

"Eight months, thereabouts."

"Hmm. And Dan Mowena, do you know him as well?"

"The Magistrate?"

"Well."

"Why not? Yes. Very well."

"That will be all, Mr Shechem. You are a free man… and please accept the apologies of the Ministry for all the abuse. Arrangements are being made for reparation."

Shechem did not rise or respond. He just sat where he was, as if the man's words had been meant for somebody else, somebody whose presence his stunned eyes could not see.

"Mr Nu'mvi you are a free man," the man repeated, pressing on each word.

"And the trial?"

"It has just taken place."

"Just taken place?" Shechem spurted, incredulous. "And Motine Swaibu? No confrontation?"

The man in the black gown did not answer. Instead, he leaned backwards on his chair and opened his mouth to a voluminous laughter before returning to position again.

"Confrontation. You are right. There should be one."

"I've been burning for one," Shechem said, in a voice tinged with disappointment.

"And so have we."

We…we, he reflected at the same time as he was thinking of what next to tell this enigmatic man before him. Who was he? And the we, who were they? Could this be another of Dan Mowena's ploys? What was all this business of saying he was free when in all evidence no trial had taken place? Who exactly was this man and what was he up to?

"And who are you, if I may ask?"

"Never mind who I am. Just know that we too have been eager for a showdown with Motine Swaibu and his ilk."

"But my own eagerness is dictated by justice," Shechem said, almost shouting.

"And so is ours," the man said, riding comfortably on the crest of Shechem's growing confusion. "But rest assured, we have had it."

The man's equivocations were beginning to get under Shechem's skin.. By saying they had had it, did he mean they had actually had a confrontation with Motine Swaibu? Where? And how could such a confrontation take place in his absence? Motine Swaibu and his ilk. What did that ilk imply? Had Motine Swaibu now become the symbol of something against which the law had raised its hand?

"I would appreciate knowing who you are," Shechem pressed on, without much conviction.

"Not now. It is neither necessary nor opportune," the man retorted, then added with authority: "Mr Shechem, this exchange has come to an end. Here is your warrant of release. Please wait outside for your belongings." At this the man rose and waved him towards the door.

A sudden gush of activity had seized the courtyard, so that as Shechem emerged from his trial, a feeling overwhelmed him of being thrown into an arena of searching eyes and clawing hands. People were milling about, most of whom he did not know, but some whose faces carried a vague familiarity. They surged forward and pressed in his direction.

The sun was stationed overhead and its rays were beating the ground with unusual harshness. The clerk who had stood watch at the office door all through the trial burst forward and caught Shechem by the hand and led him towards the shade of the big tree. Other people followed, and soon they were ringed by a handsome crowd. Just then a voice rose from behind the crowd shouting "Make way! Make way!" A path was broken in the crowd and a warder marched a detainee forward. The detainee moved up and placed a bundle of assorted things at Shechem's feet in a wordless gesture of obedience, then edged backwards, avoiding his gaze, turned, and fell in steps again in front of the warder. The crowd closed up as he was led away.

"My things," Shechem declared. "It means I am really free."

"But you are," the clerk said. "In fact you have been since the two were arrested four days ago. Look at your warrant of release."

Shechem looked at the piece of paper in his hand and discovered that it had been signed four days earlier.

"The two?" he questioned as the crowd pressed ever closer, as if to pluck the words from the clerk's lips.

"Yes. Dan Mowena and Motine Swaibu," the clerk said, raising his voice in a show of triumph.

A din burst and travelled in the crowd, then died down

"Those two were arrested and taken to the Capital four days ago," the clerk continued.

Just then a strong wind burst and the mute sparrows on the tree branches sprang to active life with such vigour that their shrill cries drowned the clerk's account into faint sounds. He raised his voice with renewed determination and accompanied his words with movements of his both hands.

"We understand that someone alerted the Supreme Court with a letter and sparked an inquest," the clerk said.

Angered by the ever-rising shrill of the birds overhead, a few listeners reached for stones and shot them into the tree. The birds banded off skywards, dotting the crowd with droppings dyed in black and white.

"Luck! Good luck!" some superstitious listeners said, while others brushed off the droppings with curses thrown at the creatures in flight.

The clerk continued: "For three weeks a team of legal experts investigated the Tole Magistrate Court records from as far back as when Dan Mowena became its President. The things they unearthed are beyond our imagining. Let me just say this man is the first in a series of detainees to be released. Many of them will soon follow. In fact the man who brought his belongings is also free, even if he does not know it yet."

"Teacher Efuet! That is he!" someone exclaimed at one corner.

"Teacher Efuet, yes," the clerk said.

"And the two, what awaits them?" Shechem queried.

"I cannot tell from here," the clerk replied. "All I know is that the Capital is bent on doing something to them that will serve as a lesson to the others."

Just then a song sailed in from afar, but the singer's voice was loud enough to interrupt the clerk.

"Justice! Justice! Justice forevermore!"

There could be no doubt as to whose voice it was. The crowd turned and saw Teacher Efuet marching up.

"Free! Free!" he chanted. "Here! My warrant of release! I am free! I challenge Dan Mowena to say the same!"

"And me Motine Swaibu!" Shechem chorused, rising and rushing in Teacher Efuet's direction. They fell in each other's arms. The crowd watched, some clapping, some ye! yeing.

Suddenly, Teacher Efuet disengaged and stared away with distant, ominous eyes. The crowd cut short its celebration and looked on anxiously.

"He will not get away with it," he said, resting a firm hand on Shechem's shoulder.

"If it is Dan Mowena you are referring to," the clerk interjected, "then you can rest assured that his deeds have caught up with him."

"Dan Mowena, surely. You keep my things here while I give him a piece of my mind."

"There will be time enough for that," Shechem said to the Teacher. "We've just been informed that the two accomplices were taken to the Capital four days ago."

"This is just the beginning of things," the Teacher said. "He must take full responsibility for these instances of miscarriage."

The crowd, sizeable until now, was beginning to dwindle. Shechem picked his few belongings and headed without much ceremony towards Tabi Lane.

19

Shechem did not go straightaway to Tabi Lane. Not that he wouldn't have loved to. It was just that he did not find the urge in him to do so.

All through the events leading up to his release and until now that he was walking out of the court premises his whole body had trembled with longing to see Bertha emerge from the throng that was pressing against him and soak his neck with tears of joy, with Kunsona needling from below so that he could lift her in the full view of the many admirers his dramatic release had won him, and press her tenderly against his jaw. He had thought all these things as he followed the clerk to the judge's office and then later on celebrated his release with the listeners and watchers who had gathered, first out of curiosity, then in admiration.

He had watched and hoped, on at least two occasions mistaking other women for Bertha; the first because of her dark-clean skin and burning eyes, the other for her voice that rose above every other sound and said that was a woman who needed to be heard.

He'd found Bertha's absence hard to stomach. It made total nonsense of his release. What sense was there in defeating a Motine Swaibu only to be starved of home affection? All these strangers hailing him were not the pillars of his life but passers-by who would soon go their separate ways and fall into the arms of their wives and children or drown their loneliness in beer and free women. He could not do that. He was a husband and father who loved his wife and daughter. He could not in a moment like this or in any other one behave as if all his effort to rear a happy family had only been water on a crust of deceit and pretence. If that was the insight freedom provided, then he would escape from the looming sadness back into Sanko where at least the pain would be given reason.

Bertha could not say she did not know the turn things had taken; that he'd been released against all odds and was now ready to embrace the life of a free man, father, husband and reporter again. The prison lorry drove past Tabi Lane each time they were en route to the court, leaving in its wake the surest signal possible of where to find him if she cared. Even supposing she failed to sight them as they passed, the surging grief of a wife eager for her husband's welfare would have driven her into digging here and there until her anxiety was pacified. And why not laze to the court premises, just for the sake of it? If she'd done that, she would have seen him in the heart of admiring listeners and would have joined him in those early moments of celebration. No such thing happened even though news of his release was now running all over town.

Both Tabi Lane and the offices of *The Chariot Inquirer* lay at an equal distance on either side of the Court. He ruled out going to the newspaper offices. He wouldn't want to spend his first hours of freedom in the very place that had brought him the detention. What real fun could there be again anyway in that place in the absence of Levi? And now that he thought of Levi, why not drink a beer to his memory at *El Dorado*, where he'd offered the young man his first professional break? He would go to *El Dorado* and order a Satzenbrau stout and sit all by himself and only leave from there for home later in the evening. Alcohol consorted well with loneliness, after all. That was where an abandoned husband found himself upon release from prison. Besides, he was not sure he even wanted his neighbours or anybody for that matter to see him as he entered his house. Was the place still his by the way? He could ask the same question about his wife even if he was not ready to extend the doubt to his daughter. That little thing was his final anchor, his buoy in this stormy place that Tole was making itself into. There were so many things in his head he was no longer sure about.

He would sit in *El Dorado* as a friend drinking to the memory of a departed friend; not as a husband drowning his loneliness. In his lighter moments when he was two beers or so up Levi called the bar *El Dodo*. He would lose himself in those lighter moments and allow his late friend's powerful humour to overwhelm his body.

One thing not many people knew about Levi was his wealth of humour. The thing dripped from every hole in his skin. The problem was that the holes needed to be opened by the surrounding warmth of human care for the humour to pour out and stand all on their feet jumping and stooping with laughter. Whenever wrongdoing of any sort touched his skin the holes too immediately clapped shut and the humour in him transformed into a boiling mass of rage. When Father Tinderman spat on his father's face the holes slammed their lids. When his mother aborted the holes remained shut for many, many weeks. All through their detention the holes refused to open, even once. But Shechem knew they could open and let out engulfing humour.

In the midst of all these reflections his body grew livid, as if the very air of life had been blown out of it. He found it difficult to believe that just moments earlier he had thought of *El Dorado* with excitement and even longing. Now his whole body was heavy and spiritless. He was just like a mass of dead wood; only that he was still breathing. The joy of freedom was gone.

The little polythene bag that held his odd belongings danced aimlessly by his left side, bobbing against his leg as he dragged along, not knowing exactly what to dedicate himself to.

At the crossroads into the mountain and Tabi Lane he raised his little plastic bag and caught it in his right armpit, then swung into the path that wound through the trees into the mountain beyond.

20

Climbing back to the mountain was like returning to the place of his birth. The first time he'd been there he had cast away the cowardice and doubt that had pushed him into weak decisions like running away from Motine Swaibu. The inspiring freshness of the mountain had cautioned him against repeating the mistake of the children of Jerusalem who fled from Antiochus's tax collectors and transformed her cities into colonies of strangers. He had remained up there in that first vigil and prayed, like Jesus in Gethsemane, and had returned with his heart roped in tigre-skin, ready for battle.

He was returning there again, determined to shore up strength for the days ahead, which he knew would be full of trial. The fast-approaching darkness only lit up the inner certitude of his resolve all the more. He marched up, his legs picking their way mechanically and his mind full of images of Motine Swaibu. Interestingly enough, he searched his mind but did not find Dan Mowena anywhere in it. It was just as if the man never existed in his life. He searched, expecting to find the court president lurking somewhere in his favourite sport, but no, no trace of him. The only person that danced up and down in his mind was Motine Swaibu.

He was happy to be returning to the mountain, what with the bad images storming his head, he needed calm to gather up strength for the looming combat.

Motine Swaibu here, Motine Swaibu there. By the time he returned from his vigil, the name and all it spelt would be gone from his mind and - he hoped - from his life once and for all. He would see to that. The man had been arrested and taken to the capital from where it was most unlikely he would return to Tole again. If the clerk's words were to be trusted, there was no reason to think that the criminal would survive the sanctions awaiting him in his new place of detention. Maybe the man was already even dead - firing squad or electric chair or poisoning: all these methods were inscribed in the legal instruments of the capital. One of them may have been used on him and one was now wasting one's time on a dead man. But it was always good to act from the standpoint of caution. The man could still be alive, imprisoned, maybe, just as he could equally well be where one least expected. Nothing was to be precluded, thought impossible.

Shechem settled to meditation without waiting for the moon to rise and blow into fullness. He wanted the round moon to catch him already in full effort so that he would not be distracted by the bright objects that were surely going to shimmer in the glow of the heavenly body.

He felt himself being borne to the ground and straining against the force. A figure was towering over him with two grinning rows of kola-stained teeth. The beast raised his hand as if to strike him but he parried the blow, then rolled over the grass downhill and wedged himself against a cragged rock carpeted in moss. Still the figure followed, taller, huger, more menacing. And this time he spoke, uttering fiery words in a cavernous rumble. The words jumped out fast and fled as if chased away by the sentinels of truth; fled leaving the towering figure gasping and clutching his thick neck and wanting to bend and crush Shechem with his mighty hands but also staggering with tongue hanging longer and longer out of his cavernous mouth.

The words were not intelligible because they were too loud and too swift. And they were not many either. Shechem did not overreach himself to catch their meaning but just lay against the rock waiting for what the figure over him would do. The virulence of the sound dropped and he heard money…wife…money…much money repeated again and again with no names or contexts given to them. Then the figure began to recede; and as it did so it grew smaller and smaller. First it went from its exaggerated bigness to just the size of a huge man, then to that of a hefty man, and by the time it disappeared completely it was no bigger than a dwarf.

By now morning had broken. Shechem felt behind him for the cragged rock against which he had spent the night prostrated, but discovered that rather than lying on his side he was sitting on his buttocks.

The sky overhead cleared quickly, sweeping the white clouds beyond the mountain. Down below Shechem could see Tole - a little patch of open space lost in a dense surrounding forest. But for the rooftops that showed in the early morning clearness, there wouldn't have been anything to betray human presence down there. Shechem strained, directed by an inner wish, to catch a familiar sight – the courts, the newspaper offices, *El Dorado,* anything of the sort, but nothing emerged from the blurred mass of interlocking iron sheets.

One place though that did not command his search was Tabi Lane. Maybe precisely for this reason the place seemed to jump to his notice like a pompous child in a nursery class. Each time he swept the blurred mass of zinc with his fleeing eyes they seemed to be brought – ordered really - to a standstill the minute they flew over Tabi Lane, then the cluster of houses that made up the neighbourhood etched their relief with taunting clarity. Shechem convinced himself that the whole thing was an optical illusion built from his eagerness to ignore the place. Tabi Lane wanted attention from him at all costs. And the place was right in a sense. The vigil in the mountain which he was now rounding up had been prompted in the first place by the desire to come to terms with the many unanswered questions that bothered his mind over Tabi Lane, and his own house in a more particular way. Why then should he be surprised that at the end of the vigil the object of the effort should remind him that it was still there and needed attention?

And now that he was getting ready to descend, what line of action had he decided on? Where was he descending to? Sanko? His house on Tabi Lane? *The Chariot Inquirer*? And what would be his attitude once he got to his place of choice?

Under the present circumstances, only one of these places could receive him. He reached this conclusion by a process of mental elimination. Sanko was the place he had just left. He could not return there until he provided new justification for re-admission. Such justification could come in future depending on the way things worked out, but for now he did not qualify for a place in Sanko. As for *The Chariot* offices, you did not alight from prison and make straight for your place of work, unless you were seeking a return not to prison this time but to a mental home. Home was the right place to return to. For now he preferred to call it 'the house' because he did not want to subject his frail emotions to any further battering.

Now he did something quite elegant: he decided to look Bertha's act in the face. He said to himself: I will draw a line. That at least I will do, then depending on how she reacts to that first move I could even follow it up with the duster. I'm ready to clean the slate so that we start all over. If she proves to me that the whole affair with Motine Swaibu was just the work of the devil, I will take her back and come between her and the devil. But it will all depend on her. I don't harbour any ill feelings, but I will also not accommodate any foul play. She will need to tell me clearly in her words and deeds that the whole escapade is behind her and she is ready to pick up once again with me. As I say, the choice between the line and the duster will be hers and she should be ready to shoulder the outcome of her choice. There are certain things that require bending over backward to tolerate, such as a woman's infidelity. When a woman betrays your trust, she wounds your relationship for always. I hope Bertha understands this. My detention is nothing compared to the affective distress she has caused me. I will return to her but I will be on my guard. Now that I think of it, Levi and the columnists may not have been that wrong after all. At the time I chided Tendo for his killing of the police rapist of his wife. I do not know whether I would have done so now. To stand and watch your wife being raped is one of those things no man prays should happen to him; not even in his dreams. If I feel the way I'm feeling now just at the thought of what might have happened between Bertha and that beast, then I imagine what Tendo went through in those interminable moments of ignominy. I wouldn't condemn him again this time. In fact one of the things I will do as soon as I return to the newspaper will be to write an editorial in which I join Levi and the columnists in castigating the rapist and his like. I must pay posthumous homage to my friend for his clarity of judgment.

21

Levi came round in the thick of night four days after being shot. On the fifth day the door of the brick-walled hut creaked open and lights stormed his sunken eyes. He did not have the force to speak, so he moved his body painfully forward as if he wanted to rise from out of the mound of dry blood in which he was buried.

The first warder who came in noticed a corpse move, at which he dashed his own load to the floor and crashed out, knocking against the comrade behind him and who, picking up the cue, flung his own burden at the door of the hut and turned round in contagious flight.

By this time Levi had managed to drag himself on his left side to the door of the hut left open by the fleeing warders. His right breast plate was swollen right up to armpit level and he could feel where the bullet was lodged. If he was operated and the bullet removed, he could recover and resume active life. The worst was over, he thought, especially now that he was sure the fleeing warders would alert the authorities who would come and find that he was not a ghost but a wounded prisoner whose life could yet be saved.

And Shechem, how was he? And Teacher Efuet. The two must have built a new, stronger relationship in the face of the adversity.

And Yolanda, did she know that he'd been shot and abandoned to rot among other corpses in a lonely hut? Surely, the news must have been taken to her. Now that he'd survived the killing attempt, he would give her the baby she had so much longed for. He would take her to a good gynaecologist who would detect the cause of the miscarriages. She had suffered three of them in just as many years of marriage. He would do everything to have a baby stay in her stomach until delivery. He wanted to father a child and hold it in his arms too the way Shechem and his other colleagues held theirs and made him look like a misfit among married men. But all this depended on how she received him when he returned from his stay among the dead. Maybe she would flee the day she saw him. He would have to convince her that he was not a ghost but her husband who had mysteriously survived a shooting.

Yes, he'd approached the main gate in a manner which could have left anyone with the suspicion that he wanted to jump jail. But he'd never contemplated such a cowardly thing. Jumping jail did not look like him. Such an act would not be different from caving in to evil. He could not jump jail because even in the event of success, he would be saddled with the life of a fugitive with the risk of a higher sentence if he was caught, and the permanent threat of ridicule if he wasn't. And all that for what? He would never give Motine Swaibu one minute of jubilation. The flame of guilt had to be kept burning in the fornicator and embezzler.

He'd actually run towards the main gate with the intention of provoking the team on guard to action. He did not want to jump jail but to be killed. He really wouldn't have minded dying. Sanko had become too weird for him. Not that he bothered that much about being in prison. But when the prison spun off its own internal tragedies, ate up inmates like a monster, it was better to die and be seen to have died rather than just disappear the way the others had disappeared. Too bad the shot didn't end all that agony. How could a trained warder aim at close range and do such a bad job? The overzealous warder just needed to take his time and aim correctly. But that was all behind him now. He'd survived. That was the essential thing. He would return to the worries of life. A family. Motine Swaibu. His job. Each of these compartments needed him in its own way. His family especially. He had to build one. Yolanda was a good wife who hungered for the joys of motherhood. He did not know why babies did not want to stay in her stomach. That blight will be fought. If modern medicine failed, maybe he could turn to the traditional herbalists. They wielded quite some fame in handling reproductive complications. Only that he had his reservations; but if it came to that, he would throw those hesitations overboard and surrender his marital fate to their medium.

The shrill cry of a newborn child rose to his ears even as he lay there by the door of the brick-walled hut. He could not tell what sex it was, but it did not matter that much. The cry was enough to make him happy. For a moment he forgot the pains gnawing in him and the dry blood that lay across his chest in thick dark clumps.

But now that he thought of it, the sex of the child was of considerable importance. His father…his maternal grandmother…he had them to re-name. A girl child would take the name Magdalena. A male child would be his father come back to life. He would name him Babila.

22

Superintendent Mbake Javis walked up to the red-walled hut alone towards evening. Levi was still lying just off the door and in view. As the wounded prisoner heard footsteps he raised his head with the full force that his improving consciousness could give him. The sun was going down but its rays were still strong enough to light up the inside of the hut. Mbake Javis halted at the door without blocking the light from reaching the prostrate figure inside. Levi raised his head and looked at him the way a waylaid traveller would look at a good Samaritan, then allowed the head to fall back down on the floor.

The Prison Superintendent turned round and looked behind him down the road up which he had come. It was empty. Thoroughly so. He waited for a handful of seconds to see whether anyone - a curious warder or stray prisoner - would appear in sight. No such thing happened. He was all alone with the wounded prisoner on the floor inside the brick-walled hut. Alone. He alone knew as he stood there that Levi Mu'tum was still alive. In that very instant the full weight of his importance besieged his mind. He had the power of life and death over his detainees, and he was now discovering that the frontiers of that power had stretched to include even the house of the dead. A new strength overwhelmed his person and as he looked down at the breathing figure before him he felt himself controlling not only that breath but its rhythm. He could switch it off any time, or then allow it to flow on for a period of time only he had control over.

He did not allow the burden of all that knowledge to travel too far or too long inside him. No prisoner ever entered the brick-walled hut and came out again. That was a principle known to be inviolate; and the weekly incineration of content saw to the respect of that inviolability.

The sun had now sunk completely beyond the roofs of Sanko. Mbake Javis stepped inside and dragged Levi by his two legs deeper into the hut and dumped him between two other corpses that were beginning to get bad. The other corpse abandoned outside by the fleeing warder he also brought in, then he reached for the thick, specific-purpose iron-bar that stood against the opposite wall.

When Sanko woke the following morning a lazy smoke was dancing above the roof of the brick-walled hut, carrying along with it on its journey news of the hut being haunted.

23

Shechem was still in poor spirits, degenerating physically and worsening emotionally with great speed. The furrows on either side of his dotted nose had cragged and deepened and his hair had sped up its greying and balding.

Ordinarily, his mood entered your system quietly but strongly, and made sure you warmed to it; but something inimical had happened to all that. There was no more current left of the kind that sucked you up like a whirlwind. He was now a bland sight.

He had difficulty forgetting the way he'd lost his friend to Sanko. Memories of his last days with Levi put sorrow in his chest that grew deeper the more the shooting weighed down on him. The warder could not pretend that he did not know who he was killing. He knew. There were no two persons like Levi in Sanko, no two shapes. You saw him before you saw him, heard him before he spoke; such was the power of his energy. The man could not claim ignorance. Ignorance meant total absence of knowledge...no foresight, no hindsight. This man was dripping with knowledge of Levi.

Yes, Levi appeared suddenly in his field of vision that night, and at deer speed, but anyone familiar with the architecture of Sanko - and that warder was certainly one such person for having served the establishment for thirteen years – knew that Sanko was escape-proof and that any escape attempt ended either in one of the many forbidding outer trenches or then in the barbed-wire meshes entangled in surrounding shrubs. And knowing all this, what was the need opening fire on a clearly doomed escapee? Why not just allow him to consume his attempt in one of those impregnable obstacles? What need was there in shooting down a man just inches away from sure surrender?

His body shuddered even now, many days after the incident, as he recalled his friend's bleeding body in his arms. Maybe it was the confusion caused by the sudden turn of things, but he thought he heard slight, very faint, breathing even as he bore the body towards the brick-walled hut. And why had he not drawn the attention of the warder marching him off towards that hut? Why had he not done that? Wouldn't it have made all the difference if he'd resisted the man's injunctions and instead insisted on having the bleeding body taken to the prison infirmary for examination? Why had he been so docile, so emptied of fighting spirit? Could it be, just be, that he'd actually carried his wounded friend, not his dead friend, to the brick-walled hut? Something said he should return to Sanko and ask to be taken to the brick-walled hut. He caught himself laughing when this thought entered his mind. What would they see now so many days, weeks even, after Levi was dumped there? And who would even take the pains for such unrewarding business? Certainly not Mbake Javis. Ah! Mbake Javis. Bedridden. Strong, passionate Superintendent. Bedridden. The thing had happened so suddenly, almost without warning.

His own marriage too was bedridden; but with warning signs.

On returning from detention he'd stood in front of his own house, unable to get in, until his neighbour from across the road, Ngongmun Sabitout's wife had taken up her head from her weeding and seen him stranded there and come and stood by her own side of the road.

"Your woman," she'd said hesitantly, "don go. Day you commot for prison."

"And my daughter?"

"With me. She di sleep. Your woman, she always go like dat."

"Know where she goes?"

"Capital sometime, Tabessi sometime too."

"Alone?"

The woman had declined an answer; and Shechem too hadn't pressed the issue.

"My daughter, get her up for me."

Kunsona had fled in his direction and jumped to his chest, landing so hard that both of them had tottered to the point of falling. She'd clung fast to his neck and nuzzled her head into his left shoulder. Then she'd climbed down and taken him by the hand behind the house and shown him a hole from which he'd extracted a bunch of keys.

"Who put it there?" he'd asked his daughter who'd said her mother, and that she would be gone for quite some time.

This was where he was, many days after his return from Sanko. His daughter and himself made what sense they could of the situation, but it was difficult. Gently, inexorably, his life began to feel the effects of a dreary home.

Before Sanko, for example, he'd been *The Inquirer's* accredited editorialist. So long as he was around, no-one else did the job because no-one else could do it better. His depth of insight and the beauty of his pen were still to find befitting heirs. But all this was before Motine Swaibu took hold of his life.

Since his return from Sanko, he'd written five articles. And all five had been rejected. Not returned to him for improvement. Rejected outright. In one case the thing had come back with red comments right across it saying "whoever scribbled such trash is in the wrong place."

He had contemplated quitting and actually discussed it with management; but instead of losing him to sure decay he had been handed a stint in the capital city on Motine Swaibu and his friend/accomplice Dan Mowena.

The assignment to the capital sounded quite fascinating. Maybe that was just what he needed: a change of air. He needed to see different people, different worries and hopes. A stay in the capital would help him to link up again with the joys of laughter and the charm of a quiet conversation over a drink or by the roadside.

It would be refreshing, he thought, to strike new acquaintances and begin an experience from scratch without the policing influence of prejudices or the irksome details familiarity traded. Sanko was sitting too heavily on his identity. No-one talked to him without mentioning it; no-one talked about him without referring to it.

Since his detention, his life seemed to take its rise from Sanko, as if he'd had no life before that. His total life experience was larger, infinitely more diverse, than the tiny, one-track disaster that Sanko wanted to cram his world into. He could not be reduced to just an ex-convict – an ex-detainee in fact – as if the slate carrying his life record comprised only one entry. Before Sanko, Kunsona had thrown ufos all over the place. Bertha had filled the house with song and talk. He himself had sat at his little corner poring over drafts and re-visiting old articles. A good slate that reflected his life had to carry these details. Kunsona was more withdrawn now, but she had once been charmingly noisy; Bertha was gone now but she had once been there in a way that gave vitality to his life. These were all moments he could not forget nor kill.

And why surrender his life to Sanko and its effects when in his daughter he had a stronger reason to seek a new path? A child. What greater magic of regeneration was there? The monsters of Babi Yar had not understood that. He'd combed the pages of *Grace Notes* for just one moment of relieving sanity on their part and had found nothing. Instead, he had been served tales of bestiality; of children torn from mothers and thrown alive down ravines; of children starved to skeletal ghosts; of children animalised; of children born at the edge of the precipice.

Each time he looked at his own daughter the wailing of those children of Babi Yar tore the blood vessels in his head; so that with time Kunsona came to signify not only his daughter but all the daughters; not only his child but all the children. This new awareness brought home to him his new role of father, of prototype father, with such arresting force that even the projected happiness of his move to the capital receded into a pale corner in his head. What was there he was going to look for in the capital that he could not find with

Kunsona? What? What greater happiness could tracking down the likes of Motine Swaibu bring him than a life dedicated to the voluptuous innocence of childhood? He would not only give up his life to caring for his daughter; he would dedicate the rest of his career as a journalist to writing about all the children, about their ufos and their charming questions, about many, many other things that children did and that made them so different from the adults of Babi Yar. He would write about those things so that when the children grew up they would not replicate the scenes of Babi Yar.